Praise for
Accidental Outlaws

"The hardest hitting rural noir I've read in ages, like a mule-kick in the teeth."

—CS DeWildt, author of
Kill 'Em with Kindness

"Just sh*t loads of good fun...trailer trash noir at its very best."

—Grant Nicol, author of
Out On The Ice

"Matt Phillips speaks fluently the language of the dispossessed...His whiskey-soaked prose can at times be as slick as a man slinging snake-oil, and other times as brutal as a baseball bat to the head."

—Eryk Pruitt, author of
What We Reckon

"Phillips' writing is so multi-layered and deep...An author to watch out for."

—Regular Guy Reading Noir

ACCIDENTAL OUTLAWS

Other Titles by Matt Phillips

Three Kinds of Fool
Redbone
Bad Luck City

MATT PHILLIPS

ACCIDENTAL OUTLAWS

Three Crime Novellas

All Due Respect
An imprint of Down & Out Books
3959 Van Dyke Rd, Ste. 265
Lutz, FL 33558
www.DownAndOutBooks.com

Cover design by JT Lindroos

ISBN: 1-946502-44-8
ISBN-13: 978-1-946502-44-5

This one is for all the desert rats—you know who you are.

Mesa Boys

PART ONE

"Saylor is my uncle," Ronnie said. He pulled the tab on a tallboy. Beer suds floated to the surface. "You know, like, part of my family. He's my mom's brother."

"What's he ever done for you?" Marl said.

Ronnie shifted in a rusted lawn chair. He took a nervous sip from his tallboy. Next to him, Marl reclined on a black pleather couch and chewed a hand-rolled cigarette. They were out front of Marl's prefab home talking get-rich-quick schemes. "He ain't done shit for me."

"My point," Marl said. "There it is." They both stared westward. The sun, deep in its pendulum arc, tinted the desert purple and pink. "My favorite time of day, fucking sundown."

Ronnie scraped the dirt with his Vans. He was cash-strapped. They both were, but Ronnie didn't care for this scheme. Steal from family? Shit. Still, he wondered. "What do you think we could get for that Bronco?"

"Part it out, shit. We'd get top dollar over the internet—no questions asked either," Marl said. "It'll take some time, though. We part it out piece by piece. The sooner we steal the fucker, the sooner we start making money."

"But how much?"

Marl shrugged. He scratched his month-long beard with dirty fingernails and yawned. "Ten Gs, probably. Over six months to a year."

Ronnie took another sip from his tallboy. He didn't like the family part, but the money part sounded pretty good. Ten Gs in six months. Split that two ways and it's still half as much as he made last year at Cheap Subs—fucking sandwich art. "Five Gs each, that's pretty fucking good."

"That's only one truck, too. This is what I see: we pull in a couple restored cars, yeah, the Bronco first. But then we see what else we find around town. Three, four cars. Shit, we milk that for a while and it's steady money." Marl lit his cigarette and crossed one leg over the other like he was at a business meeting or a legit sit-down. He blew smoke and eyeballed Ronnie.

"There's that Shelby Mustang always parked near Save Coins," Ronnie said.

"See, now you're thinking. But no, not the Shelby. Too rare. We sell those parts and we're done. Something like the Bronco, how that's perfect is there are so many people who don't give a shit where the parts come from. It's an early seventies model. Real cherry, but a lot of people have those models. A lot of people work on them."

Ronnie turned this idea over in his head.

On the one side, he needed cash and it had to come fast and soon. His professional sandwich artist position wasn't cutting it. And Jennie, she was doing her best with the tattoo thing, but it took a while to build a regular customer base. The thing about Jennie, she was an artist. That meant she wasn't happy doing anything else but art. Ronnie understood Jennie, so he understood that about her—he accepted it.

On the other side, steal from family and what were you? Maybe a scumbag or a lowlife. Maybe you were those things and whatever it was that went with them. Or maybe you were desperate. Maybe you were up to your neck in hopelessness and maybe you needed a little something to keep you afloat. His uncle had insurance, he'd pull in some money from this thing too. Yeah—it was all a win from what Ronnie could see. It might be wrong, with morals and shit, but Ronnie was starting to think morals were a luxury. Shit, morals are definitely a luxury. "Fuck it," he said.

"There he is," Marl said. He blew more cigarette smoke between them, leaned back into the pleather couch and smiled. "Come on over to the dark side, Ronnie. It's sundown everywhere you look."

Come down these dirt roads at sixty miles-per-hour and make believe, for just a few minutes, that you're free and everything is okay—okay? Feel the Civic del Sol slide left and right to make its way around the squared-off turns. Rattle the car's bolts and deaden the shocks across the washboard surface. See the three prefab homes in the distance, matching puke-green paint and an above-ground pool between them. Slide to a dusty stop and switch off the radio. Take one hit from the glass pipe in the center console—just a little weed to get through the morning—and think about how you're going to say it.

Like this: "Mom, I'm pregnant."

No, like this: "Okay—good news, mom. I'm pregnant."

Or, like this: "Guess what, mom? I'm fucked."

Yeah, that last one had a nice rhythm to it. Jennie looked into the rearview mirror and said it again, louder than the first time. "Guess what, Mom?" she said. "I'm fucked." Jennie poked a finger at the corner of her right eye. She had a twitch there. Started a few weeks ago and wouldn't stop. She tried to catch sight of it in the mirror, but there was nothing. It was invisible, below the surface where Jennie could feel it but not a damn soul could see.

She pulled her hair back into a ponytail. Well, here goes.

She locked the car and hurried across the yard, littered with engine parts and old tires, toward the closest house. Her mom's place. The other two points in the little prefab home triangle were occupied by renters. Her mom kept the pool clean—kind of—and the two houses in semi-working condition. She'd bought the land after winning a civil lawsuit in the eighties. Jennie wasn't born then, but it seemed like all her mom ever had came from that lawsuit—Jennie didn't even know what it was about.

She stepped over two black plastic bags filled with aluminum beer cans and pounded on the front door. "Mom, it's me!"

No answer.

She pounded on the door again.

Still, nothing. Her mom's car, an old Dodge Caravan with one hubcap, was out front. So, she wasn't at Walmart and it was too early for her shift at the diner. Where the hell was she?

Jennie pounded on the door again, but nobody answered. She stepped over the trash bags and walked around back. All the windows were covered with aluminum foil or thick blankets. Her mom wasn't a tweaker, not that Jennie knew, but she did prefer a dark little house. "What the fuck, Mom?" Jennie tried the sliding glass door. It was locked. "I swear, lady. You better wake the fuck up." Jennie started to pound on the door.

"You okay?" It was the neighbor guy, a jarhead—that's what Jennie called Marines—who owned two pit bulls. He was standing there in his boots and camou-flage pants. He was shirtless. "I heard you screaming all the way over at my place."

"Just mind your own business, okay?" What she thought, though, was *Not bad*. The jarhead worked out from what Jennie could tell, and he had some hot tattoos on his arms and stomach. How old was he? Maybe in his early thirties…A little too old for Jennie.

"Shit, you don't have to be such a bitch about it," he said. He turned around and started to walk back around front.

"Hey, wait. Have you seen my mom around?"

The jarhead shook his head and kept walking.

Prick.

Jennie tried the sliding glass door again. Wouldn't budge. She was going to have to call downtown. Maybe the jarhead prick would let her use his phone.

Marl hadn't slept after Ronnie left. He spent his night playing old school Legend of Zelda and drinking beer. Now, though, Marl needed to make some money. He switched off his television and walked into the kitchen. The prefab wasn't too bad. His grandma had left it to him in her will. Sort of a jackpot for Marl, unemployed with no high school diploma and only a few years working construction for job experience. Marl's expenses were few. Property taxes, the payment on his new pickup and drugs. Lots and lots of drugs. Marl liked to have parties at his place. But he found that nobody would come unless he had beer, booze, and cocaine. And not exactly in that order.

So, to work.

He sat at the table with a phone book—yes, Marl still used it—and a pay-per-minute cell phone. He opened to a random page and chose the first name that caught his attention.

Marliss Spaulding.

Sounded nice and regal to Marl. He dialed the number.

"Hello, Spaulding residence." A woman's voice. She sounded a little shaky to Marl—she wasn't young, he was sure of that.

"Miss Spaulding, is that really you?"

"It is, may I ask who's calling, please?"

Marl smiled. People would trust, trust, trust until they gave everything. It was funny to Marl. Dummies. "Miss Spaulding, I'm an account manager here at your bank—"

"You work for Wells Fargo?"

"I do, ma'am. My name is Sidney." Marl paused for a moment. Let the lady gather herself. "Ma'm, I'm embarrassed to say this, but we've had a data breach here in-house."

"You have?"

"Yes ma'm, we have."

"Somebody got my account information?"

"Well, we aren't quite sure about that. We just know there's been a breach. It seems, right now, like it's mostly personal information, but that's what I'm calling to confirm."

"Oh hell. Did you just call to tell me this?"

"No, ma'm. Not at all. What I have to do is confirm your account, make sure that, well, you're you. I need to confirm all your personal information. Once I do that, we can cross reference you with the breached accounts. To be honest with you, I'm just doing some basic data entry here for the cyber-security department."

"Well," the woman said. "Tell me what you need."

"Thanks for your patience, Miss Spaulding. I'll make this as fast and painless as possible. Why don't you begin by confirming your home address for me?"

There is nothing like the smell of processed meat in the morning.

That's what Ronnie thought to himself as he sliced ham behind the Cheap Subs counter. The morning shift was slow, but morning bled into the lunch rush. Ronnie would have shredded lettuce in his shoes and mustard under his fingernails in a couple hours. Minimum wage, this same old shit. Out the front window, Ronnie could see his dusty white Plymouth Road Runner. The slow leak in the driver's side front tire was getting bigger. He'd have to use the air compressor before he headed home. Cheap Subs was in a Chevron station, one of those weird fast-food and deli combinations. You've seen them at truck stops between here and El Paso, the ones that make your stomach turn like melted rubber. Still, the place got busy at lunch time.

Man, Ronnie would love a new car.

Well, not a new car, but a car that was new to him. Something that started every day and wouldn't get him pulled over for fix-it tickets. He just hoped Marl was right about stealing the Bronco. There was a lot about Marl that Ronnie didn't like—like how he'd looked at Jennie's tits the one time the three of them hung out together, but Ronnie always had beer in the fridge, gas in his truck and he was always getting girls. Dumb as rocks, but they were hot.

Ronnie finished slicing the ham and put it into one of the low coolers, a backup for later. When he stood and looked back out the window he saw a Harley Davidson motorcycle coming down the highway like a banshee. It was only a moment until he heard the engine roar into the Chevron parking lot. The rider, with long hair and a white beard, wore a leather vest with a reaper on the back. Middle-aged guy, maybe early forties. Young enough that his white beard was a trip.

Sweet. God, he'd love a bike too.

The guy killed the engine and climbed off the bike, a solid black hog with chrome pipes. He reached into a saddlebag for something and tucked it into the waistband of his Levis. "Holy shit," Ronnie said.

Across the convenience mart, Revis, the morning clerk, stopped thumbing through Playboy. "What's up, Ronnie?" he said.

"Dude has a gun."

Revis came around the counter then and tried to look out the window, but the guy was already opening the glass doors and stepping inside the Chevron station. The digital bell sounded its sing-song declaration—customer inside.

"What's up, fellas?"

The guy kept the gun between his waistband and rock-hard abs. He only wore the vest, nothing beneath, like a character from a comic book. He was younger up close than Ronnie first thought. The beard was long and white, but the color was premature. Maybe late thirties. Revis put his hands up right away—like a damn soldier who'd been overrun. "Take whatever, man."

The guy raised his chin at Revis—get behind the counter—and stared hard at Ronnie. "You stay right there," he said. "I don't want to touch this piece while I'm in here, but I promise I will if that's what it takes."

Ronnie nodded. So, this is what it looks like? To be on the other side of it, to feel like the edge is right there, like it's waiting for you to step over it, like you're about to fall into nothing and come out the other side?

"Put all the money in the register inside a plastic bag," the guy said to Revis. "Then, I want you to go into that safe behind you and pull out the petty cash. You're gonna put that into my plastic bag, too. You'll bring it to me right here—like I'm going shopping."

Revis went to work. The guy watched him with no expression. After a moment, he reached out and plucked a Butterfinger candy bar from a rack and slid it into his vest pocket.

Ronnie watched the guy.

Tattoos on both wrists, but his arms were bare and tan. The guy worked out or spent time doing hard labor—one or the other. The way he spoke though, that was something to think about. Not with the same lazy lilt most people from around here used. He spoke like a professor down at the community college. Ronnie had taken a few prerequisites there. The professors had that same surety in their instruction, that self-assurance—the I'm-in-charge voice. This guy didn't talk like he was high, or drunk, or trying to get to either of those things. Just cool, like he was doing a job the same as any other day.

"Turn your head."

Ronnie snapped out of it. He felt the guy's eyes on him. "What?"

"I said, turn your head."

Ronnie did what he was told. He stared out the window at the still-empty Chevron lot, his Plymouth there next to the guy's Harley. No cops. No customers.

Revis brought the bag to the guy and put his hands up again. The guy took the bag and walked toward Ronnie. He stopped in front of the Cheap Subs counter and tapped on the glass. "I'll take a foot-long meatball," he said. "Provolone cheese and jalapeños."

Ronnie turned to look at the guy. "White bread okay?"

"I'll take multi-grain, if you have it."

Ronnie made the sandwich. Revis stood in the center of the convenience mart and watched. He kept his hands up around his shoulders the entire time, like he was in a freeze-frame.

When Ronnie looked up, a gun barrel was in his face. That's one long dark tunnel into night. Ronnie said, "This one's on the house." Behind the gun the guy's blue eyes centered on him.

"You'll wait twenty minutes before you call the cops," the guy said. "I'll be gone by then and we'll have no problems. You won't mention that I pointed this gun at you—that's what'll keep you alive after this, do you understand?"

Ronnie nodded again.

"You're a Mesa Boy, right?"

"I am," Ronnie said.

"Then I can find you. If you do what I say, this ends when I walk out that door." He shoved the gun back into his waistband and walked outside. He climbed onto his bike and revved the engine. Then, he was gone. Ronnie looked at the digital clock on his register. Twenty minutes, the guy said.

Just enough time for him to eat his lunch.

Mesa Boy—the term meant punk, troublemaker, lowlife.

All those things.

But it also meant any kid who grew up and still lived on The Mesa, just outside town. A weird place, two miles up a treacherous curved road, The Mesa had its own legends and history. The kids there—and the other residents—depended on town for school, work, groceries, cigarettes and beer. But they were in a world that seemed all their own. Windswept and quasi-lawless, The Mesa had its share of America's meth labs and pot growers and holed-up crooks. But there were artists there too, and old-timers and young families with five-acre plots.

The Mesa and the town, their differences came down like this:

There were the bosses; people in charge of other people and who owned businesses in town and in other towns stretching east and west along the highway. There were The Mesa folks; so much white trash and second or third-generation Latinos and a few, mostly middle-class black families living in self-imposed urban exile.

Didn't matter how big the Walmart was or how many fast-food joints sprouted up like weeds in town. Didn't matter that the car dealerships thrived or that the census kept showing progress—this was a small town. And it always would be a small town. An outlaw stench hung everywhere alongside the dust; in the saloons, the diners, the tattoo parlors. That stench hung like air over The Mesa.

And some of these Mesa people were descended from goddamned outlaws and homesteaders and gold miners. A great many of them, carried a lineage that stretched back to Manifest Destiny, to a still-ongoing, brutal conquest of a land unforgiving. Freedom, they thought, had something to do with semi-automatic weapons and four-wheel drive and beer and pit bulls. Mean streaks were forgiven, parlayed, understood.

That's just how he is, they said. Deal with it.

There's a similar history everywhere you look in all the small towns of the Southwest, along the smooth, agricultural contours of Middle America, in the humid South. In the North, too.

Mesa Boy: Punk. Troublemaker. Lowlife. Even, some might say, outlaw.

Ronnie turned left into Marl's dirt driveway. He could see Marl outside, shirtless in the sun. He was putting down rabbits with a pellet gun. Marl being a bastard to the little desert creatures again, though he did make a decent rabbit stew. Ronnie parked the Plymouth in the line of fire. That might piss Marl off, but it was worth the laugh.

"You son of a bitch," Marl said. "I was shooting your dinner."

"Shit." Ronnie slammed his door and leaned against the car. "You ain't going to believe what fucking happened to me at work this morning."

"Revis finally give you that BJ?" Marl smirked. He lit a cigarette and fell back into the pleather couch.

"We got robbed," Ronnie said. "At gunpoint, too, point-blank." That sounded kind of funny. But it was what happened. "Dude took down Revis for the money in the register and the safe. Had me make him a meatball sandwich for the road."

Marl laughed at that. "No shit? White or wheat bread?"

"Multi-grain."

"Health nut, huh? You know the guy?"

"Never seen him before. He knew I lived on The Mesa though. Told me I'd regret giving the police enough description to catch him. Told me to play dumb."

"Well, did you?"

"Do I look stupid to you?"

Marl rocked his head from side to side.

"Don't answer that. I said I didn't get a good look at the guy, told the cops I was too scared to tell if the bike was a Harley or a Honda."

"I thought the guy asked you to play dumb—not ignorant."

"Rode in on a Harley," Ronnie said. "He was like a Hell's Angel or something…had a vest with a reaper on the back."

"Probably one of those meth cooks hard up for cash. Good for him, how much was the take?"

Ronnie squinted at Marl. Sometimes he was such a punk. There he was, lounging like a king on his cheap patio furniture, talking like he was tied in with the mob. "Fuck if I know. He maybe got a thousand total. I didn't ask Revis."

"How much you make today?"

"Fifty bucks or so, why?"

"I bet that guy made more in ten minutes than you make in a month."

"Yeah," Ronnie said. "I bet." The previous evening's conversation entered Ronnie's head. That was what Ronnie wanted to talk about. If they were going to steal the restored Bronco from Saylor—Ronnie's uncle—they needed a plan, and they needed a plan that wouldn't get them caught.

"It's what we're going to do," Marl said.

"What?"

"Up our hourly wage, that's what."

"You don't even have a job," Ronnie said.

"You're damn right about that." Marl lit another cigarette and smiled. He had straight teeth, not like some of the other Mesa folks. Part-Indian, Marl had free health care on the reservation. Ronnie doubted that heritage, he figured it was something Marl put together with fancy paperwork. The smile disappeared into Marl's stiff pull on the cigarette.

"Dude, when you want to do this?" Ronnie said. "You know, the thing."

"The thing?" Marl stood and walked across the yard. He stepped over piles of crushed beer cans and cigarette butts, leftovers from his parties. He leaned against the Plymouth, took another drag from his cigarette and tilted his head. "I'm ready when you are." Then, to imitate Ronnie, he added, "Dude."

* * *

That damn twitch.

Jennie felt it just below her skin, a phantom needle inside her face.

She tried to ignore it while the fat cop explained everything to her, but still the twitch was there. She stood outside her mom's prefab. Mid-afternoon and the sun was hard and hot on Jennie's shoulders. Yellow crime scene tape wrapped the house. The neighbors were out for a look—the jarhead lounged in a lawn chair and the family across the way gathered like a posse. Mom, dad, and three spit-mouthed toddlers watched the cops move in and out of the house. Two detectives—in ill-fitting Sears suits—pulled onto the scene and marched inside with legal pads. An ambulance and the volunteer fire department and a state trooper showed before them, a real big show for all the neighbors.

The fat cop—not a trooper, but a local cop with the county sheriff—waved his hand in front of Jennie's face. "Hey there," he said. "You're still with me, right, Jennie?"

Jennie nodded and crossed her arms over her chest. "Yeah."

"We won't know cause of death for forty-eight hours," he said. "When we know, homicide will give you a call."

"Cause of death? Someone fucking beat her to death."

"That's what it looks like, but we need specifics, Jennie, that's all. If you want, I can help you call somebody to pick you up."

"My car is right there," Jennie motioned toward her little Honda. "I can drive myself."

Fat Cop nodded and walked back into the house.

Jennie kept seeing the black-blue bruises on her mom's face and naked body. Dark splotches marked her mom's pale, translucent skin.

Naked. My mom died naked.

Jennie used the jarhead's cell phone to call around town, but nobody had seen her mom for a few days. So, Jennie broke a window over the kitchen sink. She saw the blood as she tried to shimmy in through the window. The blood was black and sticky and thick. Jennie thought of blood as red, but her mom's blood was deep and dark like motor oil. Naked. Her mom died naked. Climbing through the window, Jennie saw the long, thin scar across her mom's stomach. It was the scar Jennie left when she was a baby—she'd marked this woman for life, her mother.

Jennie used the jarhead's phone again. She called the cops. And now, here she was, standing outside her mom's prefab while detectives dusted for prints and looked for evidence.

Fuck me. Fuck me. Fuck me.

Jennie walked to her car. She collapsed inside and locked the doors. There was her face, it stared at itself in the rearview mirror. It was an older face than Jennie felt, wrinkled from smoking cigarettes and far too pale. "Mom," Jennie said, "I'm pregnant." There that twitch again. It burned the corner of Jennie's eye.

Her gaze shifted to the house, to the crime scene investigators marching in and out her mom's front door, to the neighbors lounging in lawn chairs and smoking their cigarettes. And then, without Jennie noticing, two salty tears rolled down her right cheek and dripped from her trembling chin.

Ronnie parked his Plymouth behind Jennie's Honda. Past her car, he could see the lights on inside their single-wide mobile home—well, not theirs exactly, but they lived in it. They rented it from Marl who, one way or the other, had a few properties he rented out across The Mesa. The mobile home was newer, not bad for what they paid, but Ronnie was fed up with paying rent. Seemed to him that he and Jennie could find a way to buy their own land. They could get a prefab home or maybe build their own place over a couple years.

For now, though, this was it. A single-wide with one bedroom and one bath, a little patio out front covered by a Walmart tarpaulin.

Ronnie wasn't sure what was up with Jennie the past few weeks. She'd spent less time drawing and more time watching cooking and reality shows. Shit, one night she stayed up past midnight playing Nintendo. Nothing wrong with that, but Ronnie could tell she was drifting. She was somewhere else, not there with him at all. Ronnie knew things bore down on relationships. He knew that not having enough money stressed them both until they were at each other's throats. With Ronnie's first check each month they paid Marl his rent money. Then, they paid utility and cable bills—two weeks late—with the second check. That second check left them with $150 to get through three weeks of food and gas and whatever else they needed. They did it. It was possible, but it wasn't pleasant. And for Ronnie, each month seemed to add more and more pressure until their relationship wouldn't hold together. Sometimes Jennie could make some cash babysitting or from a tattoo she put on somebody, but it was never enough to save anything—that was just money to catch them up on bills.

He was kidding himself. No, lying to himself. How would he ever buy land? He was lucky to have a bank account. He was lucky to have a car that started when it was cold. He was lucky to have Jennie, a girl who would laugh with him at stupid jokes and watch cartoons when he wanted.

Ronnie locked the Plymouth. It was dark out, but he could make out the Joshua tree silhouettes in the distance. The trees pointed at the sky like jagged fingers on the horizon and for a moment Ronnie could feel that firm and certain pull deep inside his chest—this was home, his place.

He unlocked the door and found Jennie sitting on the sofa. She had a beer in one hand and she was, Ronnie could tell, crying. He let the door slam behind him and sat down next to her. "Rough day?"

"You could say that," Jennie handed him the beer. "Went over to my mom's house today."

"How's she doing?" Ronnie took a long swig from the bottle and finished it.

Jennie laughed.

She let it out first like a secret sound, but it built and built until she was crying again. Ronnie watched her without moving. Times like these, he didn't know how to react. Jennie wiped the tears away and stared at the ceiling, that leaky ceiling with its brown-black circles where the rainwater pooled and seeped.

"She's not doing too good," Jennie said. "She's dead."

Ronnie felt a twist form inside his belly, a tear that started and stretched up into his heart and stretched down into his groin. He felt like cheap plastic ripped into nothing by a child's hands. Heroin—that was Ronnie's first thought. Maybe one load too many for Cheryl? It was cruel and he felt guilty at the thought, but it was a logical conclusion. "Sweetie, I'm sorry." He moved closer to her and picked up her hands. They were limp and cold and pale. "Why didn't you call me?"

Jennie's eyes pivoted to Ronnie's. The green inside them, somehow, seemed less olive-bright. Behind those eyes, something had given way and Ronnie could sense this burden hanging there in the darkness of Jennie's mind. "Someone killed her, Ronnie. Someone beat my mom to death."

The moment came down on Ronnie like a shadow, a heavy-hot blanket that settled and suffocated him until breathing was work. The moment smothered him. They sat in silence. Then, Jennie cleared her throat. Ronnie watched as she inhaled and stretched her neck. There was something else.

"I've been waiting to tell you something, Ronnie."

"Okay." He squeezed her hands.

"Ronnie." Deep breath. "I'm…"

She looked down at her belly. He followed her eyes.

PART TWO

Ronnie parked the Plymouth on the west side of the highway, across from his uncle's shop. Marl smoked cigarettes and downed cans of Budweiser in the passenger seat. It was dark, but Ronnie still steered off the highway shoulder and into the dirt. From where they were, Ronnie could see the high, chain-link fence with barbed wire on top. Beyond that was a square, corrugated metal building, the shop. A hand-painted sign on it said: "Restoration, Rejuvenation, Repair—Saylor's Auto." Ronnie could see, too, the red seventies Bronco—shiny and perfect in the night—parked on the building's far side. Two video cameras jutted from the roof. Ronnie knew the cameras formed a cross-view of the shop's exterior.

"See how good of a shot I am tonight," Marl said. He grabbed a .22-caliber Winchester rifle from the back seat. The rifle seemed small and less than threatening, something for a kid to learn with, but it was accurate. "Had this since I was a little boy. Imagine that—shooting with this rabbit gun tonight."

"Two shots, dude. Get it done in two shots."

"Don't worry about it. You know how many people out here fire shots every night? Anybody who hears will think we're playing around, drunk and shooting at the stars." Marl levered the rifle and a round clicked into place.

He rolled down his window.

Ronnie watched as Marl perched the gun's barrel on the Plymouth's side view mirror. Marl leaned over the stock, sticking his head out into the night, and sighted down the barrel. He squeezed the trigger.

A sharp crack filled Ronnie's ears and he shuddered. "That's loud as shit. You get one?"

"Hold on." Marl fired again. The noise shook the Plymouth.

Ronnie heard a soft tinkle in the shop yard.

"One down, one to go." Marl nailed the second camera with the next shot. Another soft tinkle fell into the shop yard. "Piece of fucking cake, son."

"Let's wait," Ronnie said.

"For what?"

"To see if the cops show up. Somebody might call it in."

Marl brought the rifle inside and rolled up his window.

"Nobody's going to call the fucking cops. You know what's wrong with you? Why you always struggle? Self-fulfilling prophecies. Know what that is?"

Ronnie ignored Marl. He watched the shop yard and waited for sirens. There were none.

"That's when you keep saying what's going to happen all wrong and then, guess what? The shit actually happens."

"Just don't want to end up in jail," Ronnie said.

"Fuck, there it is again. Self-fulfilling prophecy."

They got out of the Plymouth. Ronnie opened the

trunk. He pulled out a pair of bolt cutters, a slim jim and a small step-ladder. Marl propped the Winchester on his shoulder. They ran across the highway and walked along the fence to the far side of the shop. From there, they could see the Bronco inside the yard—a red, lifted truck with off-road tires.

"This fucker better start," Ronnie said.

Ronnie kept his eye on the highway as Marl went to work with the bolt cutters, but they were below the road and he doubted a driver would catch sight of them, even if a pair of headlights happened to swing their way. A perfect crime, if there is such a thing. The idea was to cut a long, wide arc in the fence and drive the Bronco right through it. Marl would put it in four-wheel drive—hopefully, if it worked—and drive up the wash and out the other side. From there, he could hook up with a Jeep trail and get the Bronco back to his house. That was how Ronnie understood the plan. It would work if nothing went bad.

Ronnie squeezed through the fence as soon as the first section was cut, reaching back to grab the slim jim. He drifted over to the Bronco and went around to the driver's side. He put his hand over his eyes and pressed against the window. Ronnie laughed. "You ain't going to believe this."

Marl raised his chin. "What now?"

"It's unlocked," Ronnie said. He pulled the handle and opened the door.

Packard was pissing on his campfire when he heard the shots. Three shots. Long, echoing reports that cracked like hammer blows. Probably a small Winchester, kids out shooting rabbits or coyotes. Not uncommon in a place like The Mesa—people could be kind of wild out here. Better check it out, though. He zipped up his fly and pulled on his vest. He walked over to his Harley Davidson and took the keys from the ignition. From his tent—his small, orange pod in the middle of the desert— Packard took a flashlight and his Colt .45.

He walked toward the shots.

Packard loved the desert at night; the quiet sounds and stillness, all the moonlight hanging like laundry. He tramped through hard dirt and soft dune, his boots like stamps against the earth. Packard lived alone. He lived in his tent and on his Harley and on the road—that was it, his whole life. Before that, there had been another life. A life that seemed too easy, too refined and perfect.

Now, though, he was a drifter.

If he'd been born in another century, Packard might have been a gunslinger or rode shotgun on a stagecoach. He was contemplative to a fault, and Packard had a thing inside him that pulled toward open spaces, toward desolation and emptiness. Sometimes, that thing pulled him toward evil, took him over an edge and into a dimness he struggled to understand. Like today, in the Chevron Station, when he'd scared the shit out of that clerk. The money—he didn't care about that, it was paper and metal and he needed it to survive. But the fear he'd created, that was evil. And Packard knew that. The way he'd pointed his pistol at the sandwich boy, that was something he wished he hadn't done. Felt outlaw-ish at the time, but it was a toeing-the-edge moment.

And when you toe the edge, there's always a chance you step over it.

The flashlight beam darted ahead of him like a bug.

He crested a small dune and stood looking down at the highway. There weren't any cars this time of night, just a lonely stretch of pavement lazing through the desert. To his left, across the highway, was Saylor's Auto Repair. The lot was empty and a security light cast a boomerang-shaped glare down on it. Those shots were probably nothing, just someone out having a little midnight fun.

He saw the two figures when they were almost across the highway. They lurched quickly past the center line and onto the shoulder, sank down below the road. Looked like they were carrying something. Packard lost sight of the men—he figured they were men—and tried to get to higher ground so he could see what they were doing. He scrambled along the dune and up a small pile of boulders—these giant, round stones that made him think of Mars and sci-fi books.

One guy was using something on the chain-link fence that surrounded Saylor's lot, maybe bolt cutters. Packard watched another guy slide through the fence after a second and cross the lot toward that fancy red Bronco. Packard saw the truck each time he passed Saylor's—a nice-looking four-by-four, restored and maintained, an early seventies model. "Holy shit," Packard said. *These guys are scoring right now.*

The guy who crossed the lot walked around to the driver's side, peered in the window and opened the door. He climbed inside the Bronco. The fence man kept working at his job. He unfolded a small step-ladder and used that to reach higher up the fence. The chain-link swung in a big loose, three-sided square. Packard smiled to himself. Not bad, pretty fucking smart.

The Bronco started a second later. It was a loud rig and the roar echoed up to where Packard stood. Not exactly a quiet escape for these two. The Bronco inched toward the chain-link—with the lights off—then, slowly, moved through it onto the other side. The driver climbed out and switched places with the fence man. He bent down at the front tires and flipped the hubs. They were going to use four-wheel drive. Packard smiled again and said, "A desert escape."

The guy gathered all the tools and tossed them with the step-ladder into the Bronco. He talked with the driver for a moment and slammed the door. The Bronco inched down the wash alongside the fence and disappeared from Packard's view. He watched as the lone figure climbed up to the highway and crossed the road. An engine fired up and Packard watched as a car's headlights swept the highway, pivoted over Saylor's Auto Repair—no longer graced by the fancy Bronco—and pointed back toward town. The car bounced onto the highway and picked up speed.

Packard knew that car. "A Plymouth Road Runner," he said to himself. "Dusty white, no hubcaps." Yeah.

He'd seen it today, in fact.

They fucking did it.

Ronnie pounded the dashboard of the Plymouth with his fist. He rolled down the window and stuck his head into the wind. "We fucking did it!" His voice hit the air like static and flew backwards into the night. He brought his head back inside and switched on the radio. Nothing but static. He twisted the knob and found whatever sound he could endure. Happened to be that Mexican stuff that always came in clear. He turned the volume up as loud as his speakers could handle. Ronnie leaned back into the seat and mashed the gas pedal down, he wanted to feel speed and air rushing past him.

He couldn't believe the Bronco was unlocked, the way it all went down so smooth. The keys were there, too, sitting on the floor like a gift from almighty God his damn self. Didn't even have to hot-wire the fucker. He just turned the key and drove it through the fence. The plan seemed to work and there wouldn't be any security camera footage. He was sure Marl had tagged both cameras on the roof.

Dare he say it again? A perfect crime.

Not bad for a Mesa Boy, a kid who barely graduated high school. There wasn't an ounce of guilt in Ronnie, not then. To hell with his uncle. He never saw the guy, anyway. And his mom? Like forever, she was off some-where getting high. She could go to hell, too. Ronnie had a baby on the way and he was tired of hustling from one paycheck to the next, he was tired of feeling like his whole life was underwater.

Now, Marl needed to get that Bronco hidden. They'd start taking it apart tomorrow. Shit, probably have half the truck listed online by week's end. Ronnie swung through the highway's curves like he was in a dream.

The one thing that bothered him was he couldn't tell Jennie about the Bronco. He couldn't tell anyone. Jennie, man, it was a horrible day for her. Ronnie tried to imagine what it must have been like—to see her mom all bashed to death. And the baby, he figured Jennie was planning on telling her mom. He understood that, and he didn't mind. But to find her mom like that?

Not exactly a warm and fuzzy start to her pregnancy.

He'd put Jennie to bed that evening, sat with her while she cried into her pillow. It wasn't a great way to learn he was going to be a dad, but Ronnie kissed Jennie's neck and told her they'd be alright. He'd have to help Jennie with arrangements for Cheryl's funeral service tomorrow and for the rest of the week, but right now Ronnie felt like things were going to shake out okay. He could smell the money in his pocket. Ronnie wanted—he always did want—to live a normal life with Jennie. He figured they'd have kids, but maybe in a few years. Now, things were jumping ahead and he needed to catch up—the Bronco might get him there. Ronnie needed a little money in the bank, that's all. He'd use it to rent a nicer place, to buy some stuff for the baby—crib, blankets, diapers, whatever—and to get a new damned car. Maybe he would tell Jennie about tonight, but later, after he and Marl split the money.

For now, he smiled at himself in the rearview mirror. Not an ounce of guilt in Ronnie. Nope.

They fucking did it.

The Bronco climbed like a beast. Marl steered it through the sandy wash and went full-throttle up an embankment. Soon, he rolled above the highway and stopped. He watched Ronnie swing his old, shitty Plymouth onto the highway and point his headlights toward town. What a fucking idiot, Ronnie. Marl couldn't imagine how Ronnie had let him drive the Bronco away. The kid would never see the truck again, and he'd sure as hell never get any money. Marl watched the Plymouth disappear. A part of him felt sorry for Ronnie, the way he always kept on about money trouble, but Marl was sick of his excuses. Thing was, Ronnie didn't know how to play his cards right. Look at tonight—he lets Marl drive off in the merchandise?

Bad move.

He'd known Ronnie forever. And that whole time, Ronnie was always weak. He never took a chance. Now, he had taken a chance but Marl was going to fuck him. Tough titty, dude.

It took Marl a while to figure out, but in the end it was simple. He waited for Ronnie to bring up money, and he threw out this idea about the Bronco. Make no mistake, Marl was going to make this thing with the Bronco happen. He was going to chop the fucker up and sell it piece by piece. But what Ronnie never stopped to ask himself: Why would Marl need help doing something he could do himself? Why would Marl split a score he could pull off alone? The answer, of course, was that there was no reason.

Unless he wanted to get Ronnie into some deep shit.

There weren't two cameras recording the lot at Saylor's Auto Repair, there were three. Marl knew because he'd scoped the place out a few weeks before. The third camera looked on the lot at eye level, but it pointed back at the shop from one corner of the chain-link fence. Tonight, that camera recorded one Ronnie Sayles—dumb fuck Mesa Boy—climbing into a red Ford Bronco and driving it off the lot. Now, why in the hell would Ronnie Sayles be stealing a car from his uncle, Saylor Sayles? Marl assumed this would be pretty difficult for Ronnie to explain. But that didn't matter either.

Ronnie wouldn't make it through the night, not if Marl had his way. This night was just getting started for Marl, there was a lot to do yet.

He tried to find a rock station on the radio, but the

reception was shitty this far out in the desert. He settled on Mariachi. That shit came in clear no matter where you were. He gassed the Bronco—god, it rumbled so fucking clear—and spun out. The truck bounced down the Jeep trail. Marl planned to take care of Ronnie, and some other things. But first he wanted to scope something out. Word had it that the cops were over at Cheryl's place today. Turned out she was dead. All those cops buzzing around, falling over themselves to find evidence, Marl thought that would be one hell of a sight to see.

If Marl had stayed where he was just a few moments longer, he would have seen a motorcycle power through its curve, glide past Saylor's Auto Repair, and shift into fourth gear as the driver throttled that puppy after Ronnie. But Marl didn't stay. And so he didn't see the drifter, with that long hair splayed out behind him and that black vest decorated with a reaper, glide like moonlight down the highway.

But that's what happened.

Packard ran, through creosote and cacti, back to his Harley. He hopped on and took off after the Plymouth. It was curiosity that drove him to do this. Packard knew an opportunity to make good when he saw it, but this was something else. The Plymouth belonged to one of the kids—twenty-somethings were kids to him at his age—who worked at the Chevron station. Couldn't belong to that clerk—no way. That kid couldn't steal a car if his life depended on it. He was soft. The other kid, though, the sandwich maker, he was different. Packard knew he had a hardness in him, a desperation that only other desperate souls could sniff out. Man, the kid asked him if he preferred white or wheat, like the hold up was a joke, or a scene on a TV show.

Packard leaned the motorcycle into the highway's curves. He pushed the machine as far as it would go, until it topped the RPM gauge along the straights. Until the rumble thronged his ears and echoed in his head. The desert flew by him like a smashed painting and soon he saw the dim blinking of red taillights a few hundred yards ahead. After about a mile, Packard made the Plymouth's rear profile and he fell back to follow without being noticed. He wanted to see where this kid stayed. Packard didn't know why, not yet, but for some reason he needed to know.

Jennie couldn't sleep.

It was the eye twitch and the raw feeling in her throat from crying, but it was these horrible thoughts in her head, too. Thoughts like nightmares that kept her awake. That sticky, black bloodstain she'd seen wouldn't leave her head. Her mom's smashed face, blue-black and swollen, lurked behind Jennie's eyelids.

Fuck.

No beer or weed for Jennie. Not anymore. That's one thing her and Ronnie talked about before he left, they were going to do the best they could for their kid—that meant eating healthy and laying off the recreational drugs.

It was going to be a long nine months.

But tonight, maybe she could make an exception for this horrible, fucked up, endless day and night.

No. No exceptions they'd decided.

Jennie got up and walked outside onto their patio, a

few lawn chairs and a blue tarp from Walmart. Not exactly luxury, but Jennie loved it. So did Ronnie. It was warm outside, still late summer and pleasant before the stiff winter wind shivered the walls of their single-wide. She liked where they lived, too. Not so much the mobile home, the thing got old. But she loved the desert and the quiet, the solitude they had each morning and evening. It would be alright to raise a kid here. You just needed to make sure that kid saw the world outside of this place. You'd go places, travel, read books and listen to music. She'd read to their kid—no doubt about it. And her kid would listen to blues and country music. Her kid wouldn't watch too many cartoons or eat too much sugary cereal, no way. Her kid would go to bed at eight and wake up to a clean home with a pancake breakfast on the table. This she promised herself.

Jennie put her hand under her shirt and felt her belly's smooth, taut skin. It was flat and solid. No baby bump, yet. She wondered what it would be like, to feel some alien thing growing inside her. She wondered if, like her mom, she'd end up with a scar on her belly. That scar was long and jagged, but it wasn't ugly. Her mom even used to swim in a bikini when Jennie was little. She wore the scar like a badge, like a trophy.

Really, Cheryl and Jennie grew up together. Cheryl was twenty-two when Jennie was born. Pretty old, at least by standards set in town and on The Mesa. Any girl who didn't run off to college usually got pregnant before twenty-two. Jennie was twenty-four now. In a way, her and Ronnie had waited.

She remembered, as a little girl, drawing pictures with broken crayons in a diner booth while her mom waited tables. She remembered spending one Christmas, as a teenager, in the Motel 6 on Main Street, but it was a good Christmas—they were together. Jennie got a diary with a leather cover for a present, something she still used. After she filled the pages she bought refills from the stationary store and kept using the cover. Her diaries were packed away in boxes, under the bed. She also remembered her mom darting out for an hour during that Christmas. Jennie watched cartoons and peeked out the window every few minutes. Back then, she didn't know what her mom was into, but she knew her life wasn't normal. Still, Jennie always had food to eat and she was always warm.

Later, after she graduated high school, Jennie realized her mom was into drugs. Sometimes heroin and, of course, alcohol. But only in the last year or so had things seemed worse. She started missing her shifts down at the diner. Jennie got calls from creditors asking for Cheryl's number. Jennie suspected heroin, but Cheryl knew how to hide things, she always had known how to do that. And Jennie hadn't asked. Maybe she should have. Jennie always thought, like Ronnie did, that her mom might die from an overdose or a bad cook. But what Jennie saw this morning? No, she never would have imagined it.

Maybe the neighbors saw who did it. She didn't even get a chance to talk to that jarhead once the cops arrived. Maybe he'd seen somebody. Or, maybe he knew her mom better than he let on. The guy had practically ambushed Jennie that morning, crept up on her in the backyard. What the hell was that about?

Jennie touched her belly again. She wouldn't mind having a scar, not if it meant she'd bring a beautiful child into the world. Her mom didn't mind the scar

Jennie left, and it became as much a part of her identity as the green eyes she shared with her daughter. Jennie needed to know who killed her mom—she owed Cheryl that much.

She walked into the single-wide and grabbed her car keys from the kitchen. She didn't turn off the lights or TV. She didn't even lock the door. She ran to her car, started it and, seconds later, the Civic del Sol careened down the dirt road much like it had that morning. The bald tires kicked up dust and the little car plunged toward the highway. Jennie gripped the wheel, her hands slippery with sweat. She peeked at herself in the rearview mirror again. The tiny patch of skin, the place under her right eye, pinched and twisted up and down.

It wasn't in her head—Jennie's nervous twitch was real.

No cops at Cheryl's house tonight.

Marl parked the Bronco a few hundred yards away where he could see the three prefabs and all the shitty cars parked outside. Maybe there was yellow crime scene tape blocking the front door, but Marl couldn't see it.

He was disappointed. What a shit show.

You'd think the cops would really dig for evidence, like maybe they'd have an investigation unit there through the night. Or maybe they'd have somebody standing guard. Not in these parts.

Marl closed his eyes. He remembered:

It was a dark, damp place. She kept blankets pinned up to cover the windows. She liked darkness. Marl didn't understand that, how she moved around all day in the dark. Like being in a cave. She lit some candles and Marl packed the bong. It was a killer piece, that glass. He offered to buy it from her—five hundred bones, too—and Cheryl wouldn't take his money. Wasn't five hundred bones fair for a bong? Not to her.

They smoked out and opened a bottle of red wine. Cheap stuff, but still. Marl thought it was kind of romantic, what the two of them had going. He'd been seeing Cheryl for a few weeks. He'd come over around midnight and smoke her out. Then they'd drink and, sometimes, fuck.

Tonight, though, it didn't look like Marl was getting any.

Marl never wanted Cheryl anyway, not really. He wanted her daughter, Jennie. He'd wanted her since they'd met one night at his pad, at one of those all-night parties he held sometimes. Ronnie had brought her by— "meet my girl, Jennie"—and flaunted her like jewelry. Something about Jennie said: You can look, but don't you dare touch. Kudos to Ronnie, that was one thing he'd done right.

Marl met Cheryl a few months later, down at the diner. Now, here he was dating this older woman, letting her rob him from the cradle or whatever.

"You can't come over here anymore," Cheryl said. He watched her sip from her glass of wine. She had her eyes closed and her forehead was furrowed. She was feeling pretty damn good.

"Are you fucking with me?" Marl said. "Yeah, of course you're fucking with me."

"I'm not—I'm not fucking with you."

"Wait, so you call me up and have me bring my weed, but then you tell me I can't come over anymore?"

"It's not a good idea, this." Cheryl wagged an index finger in the weed-filled air. "It's bad news." She scratched her head with the same finger and smiled. "It's been fun, though."

Marl took another hit. "Just like that, huh? I'm no longer welcome." He figured the bong would break, but it didn't. Not at first. Marl stood and grabbed the bong by its long neck—it was three feet tall with bright swirls all through it, one of those Electric Kool-Aid Acid Trip pieces—and swung it through the air. It smacked the wine glass out of Cheryl's hand and connected with her jaw. Marl, surprised the thing hadn't shattered, brought it back behind his head and swung down like he was chopping firewood. The bell at the bong's end connected with the top of Cheryl's head. She collapsed between the coffee table and her cat-scratched sofa.

"The fuck?" She moaned for a moment or two. Marl hit her again on the ribs and the bong finally shattered. Speckled glass and red wine covered the couch, the carpet, and it covered Cheryl. Marl sat down again and rolled a joint. He could hear her mumbling and see her trying to stand, but she couldn't do it. Marl smoked the joint. He drifted off to sleep. When he woke up, Cheryl was gone.

There were noises in the kitchen.

Marl stood and looked over the scene. He could see a trail of blood where Cheryl had crawled from the couch to the kitchen. He followed it. She was there; naked and shivering and searching through the kitchen drawers.

"What are you looking for?"

Cheryl turned around and glared at him. Her eyes were crazy and red. Blood stained her face and her nipples were hard, pink targets. "You asshole. You fucking hit me? Fuck you." In her hand, Cheryl had a thin, silver butter knife. She ran at him with her arm outstretched.

Marl sidestepped her and laughed when she fell into the wall. "You've got bad aim, sister."

Cheryl stood again and murdered him with her eyes. "I should never have let you in."

"That hurts, really. I thought we had fun." Marl stepped toward her. She shrank back. Marl thought of a tiny dog, one that barks like an alpha male, but hides in a corner when the big dogs come around. "You know how much weed I brought over here?"

"Fuck your weed!" Cheryl's head was covered with sweat and blood. Her eyes were wild and distant, like smoke.

Marl locked gazes with her tits and he smiled. He clenched his fists.

"Stay away from me," Cheryl said.

Marl started to punch her. He smiled and laughed while she tried to scream. Her mouth made choking noises. After a while, Marl stopped. It was quiet in the house. He sat back down on the couch and switched on the TV. Cheryl didn't have cable or a satellite. So Marl searched the house for money and drugs—he found nothing—and then he walked out the back door and locked it behind him.

It was still summer, and the long walk home didn't bother him.

Marl remembered. He saw that night, in Cheryl's house, like it was happening right then, like it was on a screen in front of him.

If he ever had to confess—he never would with these bumblefuck cops—that's what he'd say, the whole story. Marl opened his eyes and looked at the house. Too bad for Cheryl. And for Jennie. He felt bad about that part, that Jennie would have to know her mom was beaten to death. But only because he liked her. Though he knew she'd never liked him.

The killer always returns to the scene of the crime. Marl thought that to himself and was about to start the Bronco up again, but he heard a whir in the distance. It grew closer. He knew that sound.

A pair of headlights swung toward Cheryl's house and Marl recognized Jennie's little Honda. What the hell was she doing?

A single headlight showed in his rearview mirror; Ronnie noticed it after a mile or two. Like a flashlight beam from the motorcycle behind him. It hung far enough back, but it gnawed at Ronnie. He might be paranoid, but it seemed like he was being followed.

Ronnie turned down his music and studied the headlight. It stayed back, disappeared every few seconds beneath the dipping highway, reappeared. He was paranoid—that was it. But still, he needed to be sure. Ronnie turned off the highway onto a paved side road.

The road led south. Ronnie knew the pavement dropped after a mile and a half. The road became rutted dirt and mud. Not the best terrain for a nice bike, and nobody would use the road anyway. Not unless they were like Ronnie and knew where it led. His eyes darted from the road to his rearview as he slowed.

Ronnie heard the motorcycle's deep-throated growl approaching. He held his breath. The lone headlight appeared and Ronnie watched through his mirror as it slowed and stopped. What the hell?

The motorcycle engine screamed with a healthy dose of throttle and swung its light over Ronnie's road. It pointed right at him.

Packard followed the Plymouth down a side road that turned to dirt too soon. He put his booted feet on the ground and guided the heavy Harley down the dirt road, thick-rutted and still wet from who-knows-when rain. The bike almost fell on him a couple times, especially in the mud, but Packard planted his legs and righted it. This fucking kid, where was he going?

The Plymouth's taillights bounced ahead on the road, two red fireflies mimicking each other. Packard figured the kid knew he was being followed. Why else turn down a no-good dirt road? The kid would take the road south then west, back to where the highway split.

They kept on, headed south—a long-haired rider on a Harley following a sandwich artist in a too-dirty Plymouth. Only in America. Only here, in rural parts too unknown to matter.

The quiet and true darkness that emerged each night, that's what drew Packard to this place. The lawlessness, or the perceived lawlessness. The people who smiled with broken teeth and silver fillings. The way they ignored the cities. All the happenings, to them so far away, were just meaningless noise. Packard appreciated that—their construction of their own realities. The people who lived here, in the desert, understood solitude and patience and didn't give a damn about keeping up with everybody else. See, they fashioned an architecture for existence that ignored the grind, that lab rat routine holding millions in its grips. The slowness, and acceptance of slowness.

He'd lived in cities. For years, he'd lived in cities. And he'd held a job and commuted and gone to happy hour like a good little lemming, but Packard couldn't keep up his act—he couldn't play his part. Spiders crawled inside his heart. They wanted out and Packard couldn't hold them inside for much longer. He'd quit his job. He'd smashed his life—a vanilla existence anyhow. Packard rode his motorcycle into the desert. He'd embraced outlaw, began to live it as a choice.

Packard had withdrawn consent.

Now, though, he wondered if it mattered. Was he the tree that fell in the forest? The one nobody heard…

The Plymouth turned west down another dirt road. Packard followed, but the kid didn't do what he expected. Instead, the Plymouth stopped and reversed up onto the high, dirt shoulder. It turned again until the Plymouth's bright headlights stared at Packard. He stopped about twenty-five yards from the Plymouth and shut off his headlight. The Plymouth's headlights faded, too. Moonlight and desert silhouette outlined the two vehicles. The desert's soft darkness pressed against the horizon. These two men were on the surface of another planet.

The Plymouth's engine rattled to a stop. Packard switched off his bike. Back to that desert silence. The Plymouth's driver's side door opened. The kid from the Chevron station stepped out and leaned against the door. "It's you, isn't it?"

"You tell the cops?"

"I didn't tell them a damn thing," Ronnie said. "I did exactly what you said to do. They think I'm an idiot because I couldn't tell them the make of your bike."

"Well, that does seem ignorant."

"Why are you following me?"

"You know why. I saw you and your buddy steal that Bronco—looks like a pretty sweet score."

"How?"

"I heard the shots and went to scope it out. I watched you the whole time. You trust that guy, the one you did it with?"

"I trust him with this."

"So, you don't," Packard said. He tried to gauge the kid, see how much grit he carried. The kid leaned heavily against the Plymouth's door, like a draped puppet, relaxed. But he spoke with a toughness that called to mind broken glass and switchblades. Not a mean kid but he had a thing inside him Packard recognized—those spiders crawling in his heart. "He's going to rip you off, isn't he?"

Ronnie listened to the long-haired rider speak. The same voice from the Chevron station that morning, self-assured, relaxed, pointed and lolling out like butter across bread. Ronnie spoke back, tried to keep his own voice even and strong, but it didn't work.

The rider looked like a ghost out here, a grim reaper on a hog. His hair hung to his shoulders and reflected the moonlight into his face. It was a hard face but not too old. He wore his black vest with nothing underneath, bare arms and chest in the warm desert. And what he was saying, this bit about trust...

"What's he going to do, ignore me while he parts the truck out? Shit, I've known the guy for years. He's a punk and no good, but I know him enough to trust him, at least I do with this."

"Logic." The rider grinned at Ronnie. He shifted atop his bike and took his hands from the handle grips. He crossed his arms and leaned back, laughed. "It's not your strong suit, kid."

"You robbed a gas station this morning," Ronnie said. "The hell you know about anything?" Ronnie leaned back into the Plymouth. He put one foot on the floorboard, noted the keys still dangling like a chime from the ignition.

"And did I get caught?"

"Not yet."

"Or ever."

"Shit." Ronnie doubted he was wrong. The way he sauntered into the Chevron station, the way he made demands and scared the shit out of Ronnie and Revis, that was true outlaw—evil in the best way. "What do you think I should do?"

"He your buddy? Or just another guy you hang with?"

"He's older than me, but we came up together."

"And he lives around here, right?"

Ronnie didn't answer. He leaned against the Plymouth and looked off toward the bright moon. Marl hadn't told Ronnie where he was taking the truck. Somewhere safe, he'd said. Ronnie assumed it would be Marl's place, but now? He wasn't sure at all.

"You're getting ripped off," Packard said. "You got scored on." He uncrossed his arms and put his hands back on the grips, feathered the silent throttle. That hair again, it flashed silver into his face and teeth, highlighted his hard chin.

41

"Maybe." But inside Ronnie knew that the rider, this crook he'd run across twice in one day, was right. He's right. Marl took you for a punk. Same as always, this deal. Ronnie felt that same seam open inside him, a tear running upwards into his throat, a gully growing wide. First Cheryl died, and now this. Again, Ronnie was a fool. Brought down by a small-time grifter with a drug problem. Ronnie looked down at his foot, planted like a root in the desert sand.

No, not sand. Dirt. Desert dirt.

And that's what you are. You're the dirt in which you stand. You've never been anything. You'll never be anybody. You'll always get taken, be brought down, get kicked in your ribs. It's how you were built. You were born in this small town and nothing will ever come of you. You're already forgotten. Dead. Lost. This truth is in your bones—you're a nobody. It seasons every inch of you. This truth is the black dirt trapped beneath your fingernails. It's unreachable. You can't scrape it out. You—yeah, you, you're a nothing. Your son or daughter—they'll be a nobody, too. It's destiny. Fate. And all the maps in all the rooms in all the world can't point you out of here or away from here. You are this dirt. And this dirt is you.

"Maybe you're right," Ronnie said. "Maybe I got cheated."

He collapsed into the driver's seat. He slammed the door. He twisted the keys in the ignition and the Plymouth rattled itself from slumber. He pressed the gas pedal against the floor, a little throttle to gauge whether his heap would respond tonight. A roar raged in his ears—yeah, it would. Through his windshield, Ronnie saw the rider shift over the Harley and start it. Two metallic roars dusted the desert with engine music. The Harley's headlight switched on and Ronnie saw glaring, white light and nothing else. He shifted the Plymouth into drive.

He smiled then, a fingernail sliver smile that pinched the corners of his mouth and spread until it was a half-moon above the steering wheel. Ronnie tapped the gas pedal and the Plymouth jolted forward, stopped. The dual exhaust pipes spit black plumes at the desert dirt. Ronnie floored it. The Plymouth's tires spun like pinwheels and vomited dirt and rocks. Car and driver shot toward the rider and his Harley. The Plymouth fishtailed for a split second, but Ronnie swiped the steering wheel toward the moon and the dusty white bullet headed straight for its target. The Harley's headlight angled northward, away from Ronnie, and as his car bumped across the dirt track he caught a view of the Harley's chrome and black-solid shape. Ronnie stiff-armed his Plymouth through the vapor of that shape and into darkness—it was like steering a lightning bolt from a dark home of clouds.

In the end, Ronnie missed.

PART THREE

Jennie slammed on the brakes. Her little car slid to a stop in front of her mom's house, right next to the above-ground pool. What are you doing here, Jennie? What the fuck are you doing here? Cheryl's old caravan sat there, dormant. Didn't look like anybody had been inside—shouldn't the cops check that? Jennie stepped out of the car and looked around the yard. Like this morning, Jennie noticed the all-around messiness of the place. Bicycles lying everywhere. Crumpled beer cans. Black trash bags still in a pile out front. She looked past the house at the foothills beyond. There were Joshua trees in the distance and the moonlight lapped at the sands and cacti. This place, it wasn't luxury, but her mom loved it.

"You're back."

Jennie turned and saw the jarhead standing a few feet from her. He had a rifle in his hands—it looked like a rifle to Jennie—and he was still shirtless. Tattoos stretched across his stomach, up his chest, and ended just below his neck. "I've got a right, don't I?"

"I guess so," he said. He nodded at Jennie and lifted the gun for her to see. "It's a pellet gun. Nights like these," he gazed at the sky, looked back to her, "they're good for shooting rabbit. Get yourself two or three, shoot, you got a decent rabbit stew on the way."

"I hate rabbit stew."

"Me too. I just like to shoot the rabbits. The stew is my punishment." He spotted one to Jennie's left. It was dipping its snout into an overturned frisbee filled with water. The jarhead raised the pellet gun and fired. He missed. The rabbit darted into the underbrush. "Shit. I need more practice."

"Not a sharp-shooter, huh?"

"No. No. I drive a Humvee. This gun, though, the sights are off."

"Okay—whatever."

"My name's Dennis. I knew your mom a bit."

"I'm Jennie."

"She was a nice lady." He looked down at the pellet gun, examined it while he tried not to look at Jennie.

"Were you close with her?"

"No, just friendly. All she cared was that I pay the rent on time. I set up direct deposit into her account. She was happy about that. That other guy, though, she had him over all the time."

"What other guy?" Jennie snapped her eyes over this man, Dennis. He was a suspect in her mind. A trained killer lives next to her mom? Yeah, prime fucking suspect.

"Gangly guy with longish hair. Thing I noticed about him—he had nice, straight teeth, but he looked like trailer trash. You know the look I mean?"

Jennie nodded. She knew the look. That was Ronnie's friend, Marl. He was a lowlife. Jennie remembered how Ronnie had taken her to one of Marl's "parties." She remembered how Marl had kissed her hand like he was some sort of high-class gent, how he stood there in board shorts and flip-flops, his stomach droopy and pale. What a joke. "You mean, Marl?"

"You know him?"

"He's a friend of my boyfriend."

"I told the cops," Dennis said, "but they didn't seem interested."

"I'm not surprised. My mom was a junkie off and on. She had a job at the diner downtown, but she always ran into trouble. Most cops around here know her, or know of her. I don't think they'll try too hard to find out who did this."

"Just because she was a junkie doesn't mean she wasn't worth anything," Dennis said. "Justice is justice."

Jennie nodded. "Not around here. But my mom did good. She found a way to make her life work, even with all her problems. I'm proud of her."

"Why'd you come back here tonight?"

"I don't know…How much did Marl come over here? All the time?"

"Seemed like a lot. They'd come together in the van. I wouldn't see them for a day or two—it was like they were holed up in there."

"Drugs. Heroin, probably." She started to walk toward the house. Her keyring dangled from her fingers and her feet made little shuffling sounds across the dirt.

"Hey, you can't go in there," Dennis said.

She looked back over her shoulder, but kept walking. "What are you going to do, call the cops?"

The kid almost nailed him with the Plymouth. Packard shot out of the way, up onto the shoulder into soft dirt, just in time.

Close call. Really damn close.

He managed to hold the bike up and drift backwards down into the road after the kid passed him. He turned and watched the Plymouth's red taillights bump away and start to shrink.

Damn. The kid wouldn't come around after a little conversation. Looked like Packard needed to be more persuasive. He started the Harley and revved the engine. Still sounded like a big cat, hungry. Packard shifted into first and pointed his hog toward the fading red taillights.

Marl didn't know what the hell Jennie and that Marine were talking about, but he didn't like it. He watched from about a hundred yards away. He could see the Marine and Jennie a few feet from each other. At one point, the Marine raised a rifle and pointed it toward Marl, who froze. Holy shit, how'd they hear me? Turned out the guy was firing a pellet gun. Probably trying to shoot rabbits.

Marl had his own gun, and it wasn't a pellet gun. He held up the Winchester rifle in his hands. He leveled the barrel and set the Marine in his sights. Burly looking guy, but short. He couldn't escape this if he tried.

He swung the barrel toward Jennie. There she was— a gorgeous girl with green eyes and long hair. He re-membered the feel of her hand the night he'd met her. It was like soft velvet or thin silk or flower petals. But what he really liked was how she smelled. It was that scent he couldn't get out of his head. He tried to get Ronnie to bring her back, but the little bastard wasn't having it. Where would she go with Ronnie dead? Where would she go with Cheryl dead?

Maybe to him. Funny, the way that worked out.

Marl followed Jennie in the rifle's sights as she walked toward Cheryl's house. Man, he could end Jennie right here, right now. It'd be so fucking easy. That power felt good to him. He felt like a sniper in a war zone. He felt like an outlaw. Marl had only killed one person—Cheryl. But he felt at peace with it, like it was a thing he was meant to do. Why'd he wait so long? It didn't matter. Now that he'd done it, Marl felt more at home than ever. Man, he had a purpose.

Jennie stopped at the front door. Marl watched as she stared at the black trash bags on the ground. She looked toward the shitty Dodge Caravan and then back to the house.

What the hell did she want in there?

Jennie stepped forward, put her hand on the doorknob, gave a push. She disappeared inside the house. The door slammed behind her.

Marl lowered his rifle. The Marine turned around and walked back toward his own house. Marl smirked. He started walking toward the three prefabs and the gruesome scene of his own bloody crime.

Jennie stood in the dark.

It smelled like burned toast and gasoline in her mom's house. Who knew where the smell came from. It just was. Jennie let her eyes adjust to the darkness. Vague shapes came to her. The couch, worn thin and threadbare. The scratched and greasy coffee table. Picture frames on a far wall, the faces inside—hers and her mom's—rubbed out by dark.

Eerie silence. No clocks ticking or electric hums from

the kitchen. Jennie flipped a light switch. Nothing. The power was either cut or her mom hadn't paid the bills. Jennie took a few steps into the living room and her flip-flops crunched over broken glass. She bent down and pinched a piece of the glass between her thumb and index finger. She brought it close to her eyes. A speck of color in milky semi-clearness. Her mom's piece—the big bong—broken into tiny shards.

Weird.

Her mom loved that piece. They bought it together on a trip to Santa Cruz. They'd rented a car—thank god for Jennie's credit card—and driven up there for a couple days. Jennie remembered her mom rolling joints and the two of them laughing all the way up the coast. They listened to Lynyrd Skynyrd and the Allman Brothers— two California girls hooked, for some damn reason, on Southern rock. Her mom found the bong in a head shop near the beach. They bought it and christened the sucker in a cute beach motel. The next day they'd driven through Monterey and Big Sur, all these places neither of them had ever been. It amazed Jennie, these beautiful places in her home state, in her country. She felt an identity surface inside her while they drove home that weekend. It wasn't one single thing, or the trip itself. It was a collection of thoughts and images and the ocean noise that combined to make her feel, well, American.

That's sappy, but I miss you, Mom. I miss you.

She stood and slipped the sliver of glass into her hip pocket. She walked into the kitchen. It was too dark to see much, but the pool of sticky black blood was still there. It seemed so large, like an unexpected lake, like a sea in the middle of a desert.

Jennie closed her eyes. "Mom, what the fuck?"

She opened her eyes. The kitchen was a mess. Dishes in the sink. Cups on every counter surface. A trash bin in the corner overflowing. Blood and dead plants and dirty dishes. Jennie put her hand against her belly. It twisted and flipped and knotted and Jennie gagged.

A scraping sound drifted past the kitchen's sliding glass door. Jennie froze. A brief flicker of a shadow, too. She listened. Footsteps. Soft, but distinct. She moved around the blood puddle and used a finger to move aside the blanket that covered the glass door. She peeked through, but nobody was there. Maybe it was nothing. Jennie turned and surveyed the kitchen again.

Why the hell was she here? Was she going to solve the case?

Marl, it could be him—Jennie had no doubt that greasy fucker could do such a thing. He creeped her out the first time they met, and it creeped her out that Ronnie spent so much time with him. Ronnie didn't have many friends, though. Going over to Marl's got him out of the house. Ronnie needed that, and so did Jennie.

She walked back into the living room. The place was such a fucking mess. She needed to get out of here. Jennie walked to the front door. She put her hand on the latch and opened it. There, outside the door, like a pizza delivery boy, was Marl. He held a rifle and pointed it at Jennie. One creepy, open eye hovered at her above the gunsight and, below that, he smiled with dagger teeth.

"Shit," she said.

"You going to invite me in, or what?"

Dennis saw the long-haired, gangly guy walk into the yard.

That trailer trash punk, it was him. Dennis watched through a front window as the guy looked back over his shoulder and levered the action on an old Winchester rifle. He walked to Cheryl's front door and propped the rifle against his shoulder, stood there like it was Halloween.

A second later, the girl, Jennie, opened the door.

Dennis bet she was surprised to find herself staring down the barrel of a rifle, even if it was a small caliber kid's toy. She let the guy into the house. The door slammed. Dennis raised his service-issue sidearm, a well-used Colt .45, and tapped the barrel twice against the window.

Knock-knock, you trailer trash motherfucker.

Marl sat in the same place he had a few nights before with Cheryl. Jennie sat on the couch opposite him. Marl shined a flashlight beam on Jennie's face. She flinched and raised a hand to cover her eyes. "Put it down."

"Okay," Marl said. The flashlight beam darted over Jennie's breasts, down her stomach and landed in her crotch. He switched off the flashlight. They sat in the dark. Those same smells of gasoline and toast lingered.

Jennie could make out Marl's lanky frame reclining on the couch, but his features were obscured. His face was rubbed out by darkness, like the faces in the photographs on the wall behind her. Like her mom's face in this world. "What do you want?"

"You know. I'm sure it isn't too hard to figure out." Marl held the rifle across his knees. He tossed the flashlight aside and rubbed his hands over the gun. His voice was low and flat like an out of tune bass string.

"Did you do it?"

Marl grunted. "Your mom was a sweet lady. We had a good time together." He coughed into his fist and squinted at Jennie through the darkness. "Not the most cleanly lady, though."

"Did you do it?" Silence, the pin-drop kind. Marl rubbed his hands across the rifle. Jennie brought a hand to her belly and propped it there. In her head, she held a fear that pressed behind her eyes. It bulged inside her chest, too. Her heart pumped and pumped. Blood surged down through her arteries and back up through her veins. Sharp, hard breaths caught in her throat, but on the outside, Jennie kept cool. She shifted on the couch, crossed her right leg over her left. "You're too chicken-shit to say, aren't you?"

"All these questions," Marl said. "You're so self-centered. Usually, on a first date, you ask about the other person. You know, hobbies and football teams, all that stuff."

"You call this a date? No wonder."

"No wonder, what?"

"No wonder you're pushing, what, forty? And all you got is a prefab that your grandma left you and a creepo reputation."

Marl picked up the rifle and leveled it at Jennie. "You really know how to push a guy's buttons—I like that in a lady." He centered the rifle's sight between Jennie's eyes, or between where he thought her eyes were. He lowered the rifle and aimed at a spot where he imagined her left nipple was. Target practice.

"Okay—so you can't admit it," Jennie said. "Just tell me why, then. Tell me why you had to beat her to death. What could she have done?" Jennie heard her own voice rise in the darkness. She sensed her muscles contracting and, for a moment, she felt an uncontrollable surge of anger and grief drip into her throat. "What could she have done?" The last line came out in a thunderous rush. The twitch beside Jennie's eye jumped on her face. She reached up and pressed her index finger against the pulsating skin and muscle. Stop. Please, stop.

Marl lowered the rifle. "For some things in life, the answer is always very simple, like, why not?" He smiled in the dark and a whiteness glinted off his showroom teeth. He coughed without covering his mouth. "You should know, your momma didn't go without a fight."

Jennie rocked upwards from the couch and was across the coffee table before Marl could bring the rifle off his knees. She fell onto him and scratched at his face with every bit of vengeance she could summon. Jennie squished rubbery skin between her fingertips and felt blood as it poured from Marl's face and neck.

"Goddamn you!" Marl rolled them both off the couch and tried to squeeze his knee into Jennie's stomach. "You bitch!"

"Get off me!" Jennie found herself beneath Marl, scratching at his neck and face and ripping his shirt down the middle. His hands came down on her chest and shoulders. He was heavy and stronger than he looked. Jennie twisted her hips and threw a knee into his crotch.

"Oh, no you don't," Marl said. "Uh uh, girl."

She tried again, but he sank all his weight onto her. Jennie's strength surged and then gave way. The way Jennie's body felt when she'd seen her mom that afternoon, rubbery and boneless, that was how she felt beneath Marl—as if any hardness in her had softened.

Marl straddled her on the carpet. She struggled for a moment more, but Jennie knew he was bigger and stronger and that was it. There was nothing she could do.

"I don't want to bruise up your face," Marl said. "Okay? Now, let's just take it nice and easy on the ride back to my place." Blood drizzled off Marl's chin and landed on Jennie's face. She tried to bring a hand up to wipe the blood away, but Marl had her pinned. "Just let it be, Jennie. It isn't so bad, is it? Kind of sexy if you ask me."

Marl wrapped Jennie's wrists with duct tape.

He gagged her with a dirty dish rag and threw her back onto the couch. "You got me," he said. "I did it. It felt good, too." Marl held his arms out from his sides like he was trying to fly. The rifle hung from his right hand. "You going to take me in?"

Jennie's eyes grew angry and wild.

Marl lowered his arms and picked up a Bic lighter from the coffee table. "A white lighter," he said, "some people say they're bad luck." He scratched the lighter aflame. It lit his sharp-featured face.

Vomit rose in Jennie's throat again, but she swallowed and stared at Marl.

The flame went out.

"Tell you what. Things don't look too good for me if the cops figure out I came back here, do they?" He walked over to a pile of old magazines in one corner of the living room. "Wouldn't be too much of a stretch to understand how this place burned down, would it?"

Jennie's eyes darted around the room. The place was

a fucking mess and nobody would care if it burned to the ground.

Marl knelt and lifted a magazine in one hand. He lit it with the lighter. A small flame licked upwards and grew. Marl stood and held the magazine at arm's length. He waited until the magazine was engulfed and threw it into a pile of paperwork and junk mail. A second later, the flames were twice as large and Jennie felt the heat on her skin. He lit another magazine.

"Stand up," Marl said. Jennie struggled to the couch's edge and managed to stand. "Out of the way." He tilted his head at her.

Jennie walked around the coffee table and stood near the front door. Run. Just get out of here, right now. But she couldn't run. Her hands were lashed behind her back and the door was locked.

Marl tossed the second lit magazine onto the couch. The material caught fire and a large flame burst at the dark air. Heat and flame and the stiff little noises of burning wood filled the house.

"Time to get the fuck out of here," Marl said.

Dennis heard the lock turn.

He was about ten feet from Cheryl's front door. He raised his sidearm and planted his feet. The girl came out first. She stumbled into the moonlight and caught herself before falling. Her hands were tied behind her back and Dennis saw her eyes flash fear above the gag in her mouth.

He tossed his head at her. Out of the way. Marl appeared in the doorway next.

"Don't fucking move," Dennis said. He leveled the gun at the man.

"Hero Marine, huh?" Marl clenched the rifle and brought it to his shoulder.

"Put that down."

Jennie backed away from the men. She saw Marl's eyes reach at her and scan back to the jarhead.

"No thanks," Marl raised the rifle and stepped out of the doorway into the moonlight.

Both men fired their weapons at the same time. Jennie's ears registered the shots—the jarhead's pistol thundered across the desert—and her eyes closed on their own. When they opened, Jennie saw the jarhead topple over backwards and land flat on his back.

Marl fell into the doorway, but sprang to his feet a second later. "He fucking missed me." His voice was plain and even-toned. "He fucking missed me."

Jennie walked over to the jarhead's body. He still held the pistol loosely in his left hand. His eyes were pasted open, a hole in his temple.

"A real-life fucking shoot-out," Marl said. "Take that you stupid Marine motherfucker."

Jennie looked over at Marl. He rubbed his arms and neck like he was checking for spiders crawling on his skin. He stopped. Their eyes met. Marl pointed the rifle at her and threw the action. An empty cartridge flew from the rifle and landed in the dirt. Jennie looked down at the cartridge and back to Marl.

"Looks like it's still just you and me," he said.

Ronnie spotted the flames when he turned south toward home.

He'd checked the rearview mirror for the last few miles—the motorcycle wasn't behind him anymore. He knew he hadn't hit the long-haired guy. Whatever, that didn't matter. To Ronnie, it only mattered that the guy wasn't after him. That would do, for now.

Ronnie headed downhill on the highway toward his and Jennie's single-wide. He needed to get home. As for the motorcycle guy, Ronnie could find a way out of that later. The flames, though, changed Ronnie's mind.

He could see the fire down below the highway, on a flat stretch of land he knew. It was near Cheryl's house. Ronnie passed the turn off for home and floored the Plymouth. He turned down Cheryl's dirt road and fishtailed toward the three prefabs she owned. It was her house, he could tell even before he pulled up and slammed the Plymouth into park. Ronnie hopped out of the car and ran toward the front door. He stopped. It was too hot.

Ronnie didn't register the body at first. Instead, he let the fire dance in his eyes and draw his attention. The house was engulfed. By the time the volunteer crew made it out here, man, the place would be gone. His first thoughts were for Jennie.

This wasn't good. It wouldn't be good for her and it wouldn't be good for the cops when it came to finding out who murdered Cheryl.

Then it hit Ronnie. The body. He looked to the left and there it was. He walked over and knelt down. The guy had a pistol in his hand and he was shot in the head. "Jesus," Ronnie said.

"Hey!"

Ronnie looked up and saw a big guy running toward him. He was shirtless and had tattoos on both shoulders.

A tenant of Cheryl's, Ronnie had seen the guy around. He lived in one of the prefabs with his wife and kids.

"I called the cops," the guy said. He reached Ronnie and put his hands on his knees, tried to catch his breath. They both stared at the body.

"Somebody shot him," Ronnie said.

"That creepo who always comes by," the guy said. "They fired at each other. I heard it."

"What creepo?"

"He always comes by here, Cheryl's boyfriend or something."

"What's he look like?"

"Skinny, man. He's got greasy hair and, like, real nice teeth. He's always hanging with Cheryl."

Fucking Marl. "You know what the guy drove?" Ronnie said.

"He always came in Cheryl's car, with her in the van. But not tonight. I saw him drive off a few minutes ago, before I called the cops. It was a four-by-four. One of those old school Ford Broncos."

Ronnie looked down at the body. He looked up at Cheryl's burning house.

Marl. Marl did this.

The Bronco bounced over a high dirt embankment and onto pavement.

Jennie's head slammed against the passenger window.

"Watch your head, sweet thing," Marl said. "We don't want to bang up the merchandise."

Jennie wasn't sure if he meant her or the Bronco. She leaned back into her seat and tried to breathe through the smelly dish rag in her mouth. Outside her window, the dark desert rushed past.

Marl giggled. He slammed both hands against the steering wheel and checked the rearview mirror. "Man, that felt good. That fucking Marine, he thought he was going to draw down on me, can you believe that shit?"

Jennie looked at Marl. He had very straight teeth. An odd feature for a guy who fancied himself a poor Mesa Boy. He was far too skinny and carried a sheen of grease on his skin—it appeared he took very few showers, and rarely shaved his face. Marl was just as repulsive to Jennie as when she'd first met him. Ronnie hung out with this man. They were pals.

"You see that fucker's head? I've never seen anything like that. Jesus, that happened so damn fast." Marl checked the rearview mirror again and looked at Jennie. He reached over with one hand and pried the gag from her mouth. The duct tape that secured it to her head stretched and fell off her face, dangled like a necklace over her shoulders. "Sorry, forgot I did that."

"You piece of shit," Jennie said. "I swear to god, when you untie me I'm going to kill you." Jennie struggled against the binding around her wrists. Her arms were behind her back and Marl had strapped her into the Bronco's too tight lap belt. "You're a fucking killer. You're a lowlife prick!"

Marl slammed on the brakes.

The Bronco lurched to a near halt, but slid for some distance along the pavement. A squeal came from beneath the tires. Jennie tried to catch herself, but her body pressed hard against the lap belt and her torso drifted forward. Jennie's head slammed against the Bronco's glove box and the firm lip of a dashboard just above it. She ricocheted back into her seat. Blood slid over her eyes. She tried to blink it away, but it pooled and she had to keep one eye closed.

Marl studied her. "You're not understanding, Jennie. Did that help you understand?"

"Understand what?" Jennie leaned back into her seat again and let her head roll to one side.

"That I'm in charge now. That there's nothing you can do. It takes some people a while to understand. Do you need more time? Or should I smack you around some, would that help?"

Jennie shook her head in tiny, back and forth increments.

"Good." Marl shifted the Bronco into gear and headed for his plot of land, his old school Nintendo and his pleather couch and his cheap beer.

Packard slowed the motorcycle and drifted to the road's shoulder. He'd stopped where the highway intersected with a road heading north and south. Past that, the highway led off The Mesa and into town. Packard knew the kid wouldn't head for town, but he didn't know whether he would head north or south. *I lost him. Again.* He switched off the motorcycle and found a hard place in the dirt to set the kickstand. He settled the bike's weight onto the stand and twisted the handle bars. Packard listened to the silence around him. He swung his leg over the bike and stood, stretched his arms toward the sky.

I lost him.

He yawned and walked around the bike and unzipped his fly. He let a firm, thick stream of piss shoot out into the darkness.

A high-pitched rumble reached his ears.

Packard finished and zipped up his fly. He adjusted his waistband and listened. It was a large engine running near red line, about to top out. Not the Plymouth, no, but it was another large engine. Packard turned and walked over to where the north-south road met the highway.

He looked north—nothing. Then, he looked south. Two bouncing headlights, like flashlight beams high on a mountain, approached. The headlights grew closer and closer. The high-pitched rumble shifted to a deafening, low roar. Sounded like a damn big engine to Packard. Maybe a V 8 tricked out and tuned to perfection.

Packard watched as the headlights splashed him like warm bath water and the engine's roar filled his ears with thunderous, raging decibels. He saw himself in the eye of some deadly hurricane, a massive dust devil spinning across the desert floor and sweeping him into its eye.

The mechanical storm passed. Packard swiveled his head.

His eyes swelled then settled back into their night mode. He squinted at the vehicle headed north.

On the truck's tailgate, in big, block letters, was one word: FORD.

Marl shifted the Bronco into park and killed the engine.

They were in front of his house. Marl figured Ronnie would end up here at some point. He'd have to do it then. He'd have to kill Ronnie. He wasn't quite sure what to do about Jennie, but things didn't look too good for her. "Home, sweet home," Marl said. "Welcome to the pad." Maybe he could find a way to let her live, but he didn't think so.

"Shit hole, more like it," Jennie said and struggled against the lap belt.

Marl glared out the window at his spread. The pleather couch and a few piles of crushed beer cans dotted his vision. The house itself was peeling paint and had a large blue tarp spread across one side of the roof—that fucker leaked during a hard rain. It wasn't much, but it was his. "I love that couch."

Jennie shook her head. "Fucking disgusting."

Marl looked at her with dead eyes. He unsnapped her seatbelt and turned to open his door. Jennie twisted in her seat, pivoted her legs upward and gave Marl a two-footed kick in the center of his back.

Marl's face slammed against the Bronco's hard metal roof and he bounced back toward Jennie. A thick cut opened in the center of his forehead. Jennie pulled her knees to her chest and kicked him again like a flesh and blood Bronco. Marl flew forward and his head narrowly missed the hard metal. He turned toward the steering wheel and grabbed it with both hands. Jennie reared back for another kick, but Marl lashed out with his left fist and landed it in her belly. Jennie hunched forward. Marl's fist felt like a torpedo. Her first instinct was to fight, to struggle and twist and bite.

Fight, Jennie, fight.

But Marl landed another hard left fist in her belly and Jennie relented. "Okay. Okay, fuck, I'll stop," she said. Not her stomach. She couldn't have him hitting her stomach. Anything but that. Her baby was still coming if she could only stay alive long enough.

Marl exited the driver's side and stomped around front of the Bronco. He yanked open Jennie's door. He pulled her out and shoved her into the dirt. She sprawled on broken glass and aluminum beer cans. Marl placed one booted foot on the back of her neck. He pressed her face into the dirt, levered down on her like a vice. Jennie closed her eyes.

"That's twice now," Marl reached up with one hand and touched his forehead. Blood ran down the center of his face, down the bridge of his nose and onto his upper lip. "Twice now you've made me bleed."

He pressed his foot down harder. Jennie opened her eyes.

"No. No. No. No," Jennie said. "Please."

Marl took his foot off her neck. He reached down and grabbed a fistful of her hair. "Get the fuck up." He yanked and Jennie stood. He pulled her toward the house and threw open the unlocked front door. "Inside."

Jennie stepped into the dark.

Packard pulled up his Harley a few hundred feet past the dirt driveway. He reached into a saddlebag and pulled out his gun, the Colt .45. A damn good gun. Packard was a decent shot, but he was no Wild Bill. Mostly what he used the piece for was to scare the shit out of people.

He shoved the gun between his left hip and the waistband of his Levis. He headed straight through the desert toward the boxy shape of a prefab home in the distance. Near the prefab, Packard heard the Bronco's engine sputter and die. He continued toward the now-absent sound through cacti and yucca plants.

Packard was going to meet this other guy, the one ripping off the kid.

He waded through soft sand and crept closer through a few scattered Joshua trees. He spotted the Bronco and moved forward. The guy was parked out front of a prefab home flanked by piles of crushed beer cans. There was a shitty couch in the front and a new pickup truck parked on one side of the house.

A little farther and Packard saw a woman in the passenger seat, too. He watched as the guy jumped out of the truck and threw the woman into the dirt. Her hands were lashed behind her.

A second later they were both walking into the house. The door slammed.

Packard had a bad feeling about this situation. He walked over to the Bronco and peered inside through the passenger's side window. There was a Winchester rifle propped up in the back seat.

A door opened at the house. Packard ducked down and knelt next to the Bronco. Footsteps approached and the driver's side door opened. Packard heard scraping sounds. The door slammed and the footsteps headed back toward the house. Packard stood and watched Marl walk into the house and slam the door. He carried the Winchester rifle over his shoulder like a marching soldier.

What about the girl?

Packard knew this was something besides a stolen truck and a minor score for some Mesa boys. No, Packard saw something here. He saw it, but he wasn't sure exactly what it was. He stared hard at the house. Packard felt those spiders crawling in his chest again, the scurry in his heart that signaled a change.

It's time to make some noise.

He walked around the Bronco and started toward the

house. He slid the oily Colt .45 from his waistband and held it loosely against his side. Maybe around back there was another way to get inside.

Come down this highway at ninety miles-per-hour and make believe that everything will be okay—okay? Feel the Plymouth Road Runner sway and rattle against the steep angles of pavement dipping through desert. Feel the old dead shocks and struts twist and then settle the dusty car like an insect into the long high-speed flats. Feel the near-flat front tire hold itself together by sheer luck. Feel the cool wind and moonlight dance on a forearm and fluttering hand that hang outside the driver's side window.

See the turn for Marl's place.

See it and make that turn so fast and so pure—even with that near-flat tire—that a team of Plymouth engineers smile from the depths and darkness of their graves. Rattle the Plymouth down the dirt road and slide to a dusty stop next to a stolen Ford Bronco. Slam the Plymouth into park, kill the engine, and look at yourself in the rearview mirror.

Think about what you're going to do.

Kill him. Kill Marl.

Jennie shifted in a hard-backed chair. Her ass and her back hurt.

She stared across the kitchen table at Marl. A dim light shone on them. It cast a tired hue on Marl's kitchen; the sink full of dishes, the beer bottles left like toys on the counters and table. Jennie's hands were still bound with duct tape and her mouth bled in little spurts. She tried not to swallow the blood.

Marl set his rifle on the table and leaned back into his chair. He settled his eyes on her. He was bleeding, too. Blood caked his face and the sides of his neck. Those tracks where Jennie's sharp fingernails had scratched into him still oozed. Strands of his greasy hair clung to his skin in clumps. "Long night," he said.

"You know you killed a Marine, right?"

"Not much of a Marine. He missed me from ten yards out."

"They'll find out it was you. And then you'll go to prison. My mom was one thing, nobody cares about a junkie, but a Marine? Everybody in town will care about that and you know they will." Jennie watched Marl's eyes pinch inward toward his nose. His thin lips bent toward his chin.

"Shut up."

"I guess I don't need to tell you that. You know it as well as me."

"What, some hot shit cop is going to care about a junkie? I doubt it. A woman like your mom dies, you know what people say? Good-fucking-riddance. Out here, we call that a blessing in disguise. And the Marine? Shit, that's self-defense—am I right? Some Marine. Couldn't even plug a lowlife with a .45." Marl picked up the rifle and steadied it on his shoulder. He pointed it at Jennie's head.

In her mind, Jennie saw the bullet speed down its oily groove, its dark tunnel, and spit at her across the kitchen table. She saw the bullet peel back layers of her skin as it entered her head. She saw the bullet burrow through her skull bone and implant itself like a tick in her brain. And she saw the dizzy fireworks show that was her synapses firing for the final time. She saw herself die in a blaze of white light and heat under a tired yellow hue that made the world look dim and dirty. She pictured this, but it's not what happened. "I want to know why you killed my mom."

Marl stared at her through the rifle's sights. "I thought I might like it. And I did. Sometimes there are no reasons for a thing. It just is. It's out there for the taking."

"No. That's wrong. There's always a reason."

"You're sure?"

"Positive."

Marl closed one eye. He centered his aim on the middle of Jennie's forehead. "And what's the reason for all this? Can you tell me why we're here, what led us to this place—this shit hole?"

"Chance and choice, a little bit of both," Jennie said.

Marl slid his index finger along the trigger's slim curve. "That's not an answer. It can't be both."

"An answer for an answer," Jennie said. "You give me one and I'll give you one." She shifted again in the hard-backed chair. Her hands were numb. Her ass was numb. Her lips were bloody and swollen.

"She said she didn't want me anymore." Marl's finger slid, again, along the trigger's curve and he grinned. "I figured I'd take my last bit of pleasure right then. Get my rocks off one last time. Now, I'm about to do you."

Jennie clenched her jaw. She straightened up and started to speak. That's when they heard the drone of an engine and the familiar sound of a car outside sliding to a stop.

Marl lowered the rifle.

From outside, they heard Ronnie's voice, "Marl, you motherfucker—I'm coming in there!"

Marl raised the rifle. He closed one eye and glared through the gunsight at the smooth spot in the middle of Jennie's forehead.

The door wasn't locked.

Ronnie ran inside and looked around. There was a light on in the kitchen and he headed toward it. "Jennie?" There she was, his girlfriend. His pregnant girlfriend. "What is this?"

"I'm okay, Ronnie."

Marl spoke, "What does it look like?"

Ronnie swiveled his head. He saw Marl pointing the Winchester at Jennie and he saw the blood on Marl's face and neck, but none of it made sense to him. "What is this?" he repeated.

Marl grinned. "Mr. Dumbfuck, just like always."

"He killed my mom," Jennie said, "and now he wants to kill me."

Marl shrugged. The grin stayed on his face. "More or less."

Ronnie swiveled his head back to Jennie. Her mouth was bloody and she looked tired, more tired than he'd ever seen her. His eyes drifted down to her belly.

Jennie bent her neck and caught Ronnie's gaze. "I'm fine."

They were thinking the same thing. The baby.

"Did you think I'd really let you score with me?" Marl said.

Ronnie turned his attention to the lowlife motherfucker with the rifle. "I guess that was foolish, huh?"

"Yeah, it was. But that's not unlike you."

Ronnie nodded. "I think you should put that rifle down."

"No, not going to happen. You know how stupid you are? There's another camera at Saylor's, a third one."

"You didn't shoot a third one," Ronnie said.

"Nope. I did not."

"You were going to let me take the fall for the Bronco."

Marl laughed. The laugh was maniacal, a half-howl that sounded hollow and desperate. "No. I'd never let a friend go down. Of course not, Ronnie." Marl turned in his chair and aimed the rifle at Ronnie's chest. "I was going to kill you, dude. I was going to shoot you tonight and bury you out in the desert."

"All these years. That's what I get."

Marl raised his eyebrows and smirked. "All these years. That's exactly what you get. It's not my fault you're a damn fool. That's your own fault."

"Where's the camera?"

"On the fence. In the corner. It records the whole lot and the shop front."

Jennie cleared her throat. "What did you do, Ronnie?"

"I was going to tell you about it," he said. "Later, afterwards."

"What? Tell me now."

"We stole a truck."

"From your uncle Saylor?"

Ronnie nodded and looked at Jennie.

Marl laughed at them both, but he kept the rifle trained on Ronnie.

69

"We need the money."

Jennie said, "You don't have to do things like that, Ronnie. Not for me you don't. You don't have to live like him." She motioned toward Marl.

Ronnie looked back to the rifle pointed at him.

Marl's eyes darted from Ronnie to Jennie and back again. "That's so damn sweet. Two little lovebirds. I bet you two want to be buried together, that right?" His index finger tightened on the trigger, pressed firm into the oily moon-sliver that told the bullet it was okay to leave its home. Marl's brow scrunched into a wrinkled landscape. Time to end this, right now.

Thunder smacked Ronnie's ears and he fell to his knees. Jennie toppled onto the dirty linoleum floor.

Thunder smacked again.

And again.

Ronnie looked at Jennie. He saw her on the floor and crawled toward her. His ears hummed and he noticed a human shape plummet to the floor and lie still. Ronnie stopped. He looked at the shape. It was Marl. Marl's bloody mug, turned against the floor, faced Ronnie. The almost-dead man's mouth was frozen in an O shape and blood slowly pooled around him. Marl's eyelids fluttered, froze.

Holy shit, dude.

Ronnie climbed to his knees. He stood. He ran over to Jennie and lifted her off the floor, held her. "I'm sorry," he said. He touched her mouth and brought her head to his chest.

"You fucking better be."

Ronnie turned around and there he was, the long-haired rider, a large shadow of a man staring at them. "You?"

"That's right," Packard said. He stepped into the kitchen light and waved a pistol at Marl's body, limp and lifeless on the floor. "I thought you trusted him?" He shoved the pistol back into his waistband.

"I did."

"And now," Packard said, "you learned your lesson."

Ronnie nodded. Jennie stared past him at the large man with blue eyes. He stood over the kitchen like a shadow. She felt the corner of her eye twitch again. Jennie turned from the shadow man and looked down at Marl's body on the floor.

The bastard was dead.

Her eye twitched once more. After that, it never happened again.

Packard shifted into fifth gear out on the highway.

He leaned into a curve, pressed the handlebars against the turn and bit his bottom lip. His beard and long hair waved like confetti and the Harley Davidson yawped a dog-like howl beneath him. The sun lifted its eyelid on the horizon, along the ragged fringes of desert. A bright yellow razor-slit of light bathed the highway as the drifter with a reaper on his back fled the desert he loved.

He'd buried the body as deep as he dared and nobody would ever find it.

And maybe, if Packard kept his wrist rolled back on the throttle and his blue eyes squinting into the wind, nobody would ever find him, either.

* * *

Ronnie parked his Plymouth outside Saylor's Auto.

It was a hot afternoon in the desert. Beneath his mustard-stained polo shirt, sweat ran down Ronnie's stomach. He stared through his windshield, across the dirt lot, at the red Ford Bronco. He climbed out and untied his Cheap Subs apron. He tossed the apron into the Plymouth and slammed the door—fucking sandwich art.

Ronnie went into the office and tapped his knuckles on an oil-splattered desk. His uncle, Saylor, looked up from an invoice. He peered over a set of reading glasses at his shit-for-brains nephew. "You're four minutes late," he said.

"I'm sorry. I got a flat tire. Had to put some air in." Ronnie sat down and met eyes with Saylor. "It won't happen again."

"Better not. Boy, you got a lot of trouble to work off. You know how much that fence is gonna run me? Shit. I told you to patch that damn tire. You ever gonna listen to a thing I say?" He looked back at his invoice and waved Ronnie out the door. "You wash that Bronco first, since it's your favorite. Then you can sweep out the shop. Get to work. I need it all done by eight."

"Yes sir." Ronnie walked out of the office and into the sunlight.

Jennie heard the knock on the door, pushed herself forward until she was perched on the couch's edge. Morning sickness, she had it bad. "Hold on a second," she said. She walked to the door, moved aside the curtain and peered through the trailer's front window. "Okay, hold on." She opened the door.

It was Fat Cop, the guy who questioned Jennie after her mom's death. "What do you want?"

"I've got some news for you, Jennie. It's about your mom."

"Yeah?" Jennie leaned against the door frame and waited. They couldn't tell her anything she didn't already know, but like most things in life, you just have to go through with it.

"We think we know who did it. In fact, we're pretty sure." He pulled a small notebook from his breast pocket and flipped it open. He tapped his finger on the notepad and looked up at Jennie. "Guy named Marl Sims—ever heard of him?"

Jennie nodded. She tried to let tears well up in her eyes, but it wouldn't happen. "He used to be a friend of my boyfriend's. They don't spend time together anymore, though."

"You surprised?"

Jennie shook her head. "No. I won't get my mom back. Surprise is something too damn nice to feel right now."

"Well, maybe this'll surprise you, but it won't be too nice," Fat Cop said. "Marl Sims is missing. Seems like he disappeared right into thin air. His place is all cleaned up, but nobody's heard from him in a few weeks now. You know anything about that?"

"Not a damn thing."

Fat Cop stared at her and bit his lower lip. "You know, most folks get pretty upset when I tell them who killed their loved ones, or how it happened, or anything like that. Seems odd, you don't even flinch."

"I don't know where Marl is. Plus, I've got other things to worry about." Her hand went to her belly and rubbed.

"Like what?"

Jennie stared hard at Fat Cop and flattened her lips. She waited for a moment before she said it, but then she let it out. "I'm pregnant."

Fat Cop closed his little notebook and shoved it into his pocket. He stepped backwards into the dirt and tipped his hat. The sun hit his shoulders and reflected off his gold badge. Behind him, Joshua trees reached toward the dead-blue sky like twisted fingers pointing at shapes in the clouds. Fat Cop lifted his chin, grinned. He said, "Congratulations."

The Feud

By the time Rex got home from work, darkness lay in thick folds across the desert. Night shrugged itself over the landscape like a plastic sheet draped across a dead body. Rex worked all day and went home to darkness, nothing but beer and cigarettes waiting for him. He parked his green Toyota on the dirt front yard and let himself into the house.

He kept a clean place with his roommate, Lou. They weren't slobs and that made it alright to bring ladies back to the house on weekends—if Rex had the energy.

He did what he wanted and nobody could tell him any different.

That is, besides at work.

Rex hated authority. He understood it, knew why it was there, but he never could get around to liking it. That kind of thing—some deep rage he didn't understand—ran in his family, or so his uncles always told him. And Rex got that streak, too.

Inside the house, he grabbed a beer. Lou was out in the backyard lighting a small fire. Rex opened the sliding glass door, walked onto the porch and tossed the bottle cap from his beer at Lou, who squatted next to the flames. "What you up to?"

Lou pointed his chin at a white, five-gallon bucket and tossed another two-by-four on the fire. Flames bit at the wood, crackled. "Look inside."

Inside the bucket, Rex saw shiny white golf balls piled atop each other like round dimpled eggs. The bucket was full—Rex figured a haul like that cost a decent penny. He knew golf to be an expensive sport. He thought it more for show than sport. Shit, you didn't even breathe hard on a golf course. "Nice. Where the hell you get these?"

Lou tipped a beer to his lips and swallowed. "Was driving home out there on Canyon Crest. Came across that bucket near Flat Rock Lookout. I shit you not. Some punk was out there hitting the suckers into the canyon. Not sure why, but he left 'em there."

Rex looked from Lou to the bucket. "You got a plan of some sort?"

Lou stood and went through a side door into the garage. Rex stared at the sky and tried to count the stars. Too many, way too many. It looked like God dropped a million golf balls and they were falling right onto the desert. Rex's fatigue from the long day at work made his muscles quiver, spread a sort of half-burn through him he couldn't shake. Nothing like working in a lumber yard to build the biceps, get you ripped for the ladies.

That's what he told himself, but it was a lie.

Lou came back with an old golf club, what Rex knew was called an iron. The club was too short for Lou, but he squared up and took a few practice swings. The way he did it wasn't quite right. Lou scratched his mustache and squinted his dark brown eyes. He swung his hips back and forth over bare feet and raised one knee. He took his cuts about waist high, like he was swinging a baseball bat. "See that?"

"You're not batting lead-off. It's golf—a gentleman's sport."

"You ever played, Rex?"

Rex finished his beer and set it down on the cement patio. Lou handed the club over and Rex took a few practice swings. "Nope. Not unless you count the miniature kind. I'm pretty good at that."

"Shit, last time you were too drunk," Lou said. "That girl, what's her name?"

"Gladis."

"Yeah, Gladis. She beat you, didn't she?"

"We weren't keeping score." Rex handed the club back to him. She did beat him, but he wasn't about to admit that. Hell, no.

Lou laid the club on his shoulder and walked over to the bucket. He took one ball out and set it on the dirt. He picked it up again and used the club to scrape away some dead twigs and a few small rocks. He put the ball back in the dirt and said, "Watch this." Lou lined up and stomped the dirt like he was stepping into a batter's box. He held the club out like a rifle and aimed into the dark. He brought it down and lined it up with the ball. "Here goes."

"Don't miss it. You'll look like a fool."

He swung and connected. The ball shot off and they watched it for a moment. Rex lost sight of it in the stars and darkness. A soft plop sounded somewhere out in the desert. "Nice."

"Let me hit another one." This one curved to the right and sounded a distant slap, a hard object smacking wood a couple hundred yards down the road. "Hit something. I just don't know what." He squinted into the dark, shook his head.

"My turn." Rex took the club and placed a ball in the dirt. He took a few more practice swings. He was taller than Lou and bent at the knees to make the club scrape the ground. "This club is for kids or something."

"Nope, you're just a freak."

Rex flipped Lou off and shook his head. "You bastard." He stepped forward and lined up a shot. He missed on the first swing; the club didn't touch the dirt and the little white golf ball moved forward a few inches from the wind he generated above it.

"You dumb ass," Lou said. "Who's the fool now?"

On the next swing, Rex connected pretty good. The ball carried upward, a small, circular cloud rising against the darkness, and veered right. They heard that same slap, but it came twice, the first one louder than the second. "Probably Johnny's pad. We better aim somewhere else or we're gonna break one of his windows."

"My turn." Lou held out his hands and grinned. Rex handed him the club and stood back to watch. This time, Lou angled more to the right after he set down his golf ball. "See if we can't get us a window." As he reared back to swing, a gunshot sang in the dark and silent desert. The shot smacked against a Joshua tree and made a sound like a hammer on a cinder block. The echo spun outward into the night.

"Holy shit," Rex said, "we better get inside." He stepped toward the sliding glass door and squinted at the small square shapes of homes in the distance. It was Johnny alright, and Johnny didn't fuck around—not one bit.

Lou lined up his next shot. He shouted into the

darkness, "Take this, you bastard!" He swung and the ball flew straight and true, a laser beam Rex's eyes couldn't follow, and smacked against Johnny's house.

A second shot sounded, but missed everything. Rex and Lou darted inside and fell into the cracked pleather sofa. They laughed, but got quiet when a third shot chinked off a piece of metal in the front yard. "Your truck?"

Rex grimaced. "I hope not."

They opened the front door, stepped into the yard and peered into the darkness. The two houses across the street were dark, abandoned by even the squatters. Lou and Rex listened for another shot, but nothing came. Johnny's house was down the street a couple hundred yards, a faint beige square outlined in the darkness. "That guy doesn't play around," Rex said. "He takes this kind of shit serious, like, to the core."

It was only them up this way—Johnny and his sister Lorrie with their little brother whose name Rex couldn't remember. And it was Lou and Rex. They liked it because they could do what they wanted, except maybe pelt Johnny's pad with golf balls. Plus, rent was a few hundred dollars a month and they could play music loud as hell.

"He probably has some night vision goggles. They sell some over at the swap meet." Lou kneeled in the dirt and peered through the chain-link fence that encircled the dead lawn and dirt yard. "Don't worry, he wouldn't shoot us in cold blood."

They moved back into the house, closed the door and locked the deadbolt. Lou turned on the stereo and Rex popped a couple more beers.

"How was work?"

"Alright, same old shit," Rex said.

"You pick up any more shifts?"

"I got one on Saturday, early morning."

"Nice," Lou turned the volume up and they bobbed their heads to the whirling, screechy guitar sounds coming through the speakers. Outside, in the backyard, the little bonfire burned out on its own. There was no more gunfire.

"Hey, Mom."

"That you, Rex?"

"Yes, m'am. It's me."

"Well, about time I heard from you."

Rex pulled the phone away from his face. He shook his head for about thirty seconds while his mom yelled over the line, caught him up on family news. He pressed the receiver back to his mouth, cut her off as fast as possible. "I just called to see how you were doing, Mom. That's all it is."

"You hear about your uncle?"

"Which one?"

"Ronnie. He got into some trouble boy, let me tell you."

"That don't surprise me."

"Well, you stay out of trouble. You hear me? No boy of mine falls in against the sheriff—I won't stand for it."

Rex leaned against the refrigerator. He propped the phone between his shoulder and ear, tapped the counter with his fingertips.

"See, we're working people. That's what we do for our money," she said. "We work and we work and we work, you know?"

Rex nodded to the empty kitchen and said, "I do. Yeah, I get it."

"How's work going for you? They got you working full hours now?"

"Some weeks. I got extra shifts on the weekends if I want some."

"There you go." She coughed into the phone.

Rex pulled his ear away for a moment, pressed it back to the receiver. He dropped his open palm on the counter once, twice. He ran his eyes over the digital clock on the stove. Figured he'd try to make this ten minutes. "You smoking still, or what? I know what that doctor said."

"You know how old I am?"

"Twenty-nine."

"Shit—in my damn sixties. I want to smoke, I'm gonna smoke."

"It's your ass."

"Sure is." She coughed once more.

"How's Maddy, Mom?"

"Your sister ran away."

"What? The fuck you mean?" Over the line, Rex heard his mom scoff, like a fly got caught in her throat. He closed his eyes. Here it came.

"You gonna cuss at me now? That how you treat your mother?"

"I'm sorry. You surprised me is all."

"Surprise, surprise. Imagine how surprised I am to hear my own son swear at me. You take that deposit to the bank."

"I said I'm sorry."

"Well."

"I am."

"It's that boy from down the street again. The two of them ran off together. I don't know where. Just up and left. No note, no card, no nothing. One day she took me down to Walmart, the next day she was gone. Like that, see."

Rex ran his eyes over the digital clock again. Four minutes. That was as far as he could get. No more. "Shit," he said. "I guess they like each other."

"That's one way to put it."

"I got to go, Mom."

"You hear from your father? He send you a birthday card?"

Rex squeezed his hand into a fist, dropped it like a hammer on the counter. "Nope, haven't heard from him. Don't expect to, not anytime soon." And maybe not ever.

"Alright, sweetie. Work hard now."

"I will."

That was it. They hung up.

Garrett slid his mud-flecked, blue Sentra to a halt cross-ways in Johnny's driveway. Dust kicked up in the slight wind and drifted over the house's red-tiled roof. He didn't leave any room for other cars and, right there, that got Johnny pissed. *That son-of-a-bitch, the hell he think he is?* He didn't like Garrett, not one bit. Not since Garrett shot a tabby cat with a pellet gun in third grade. Might have seemed like innocent kid stuff back then, but Johnny thought it was on purpose and it was meant to hurt.

Johnny tapped his boots against the porch's wood floor and sipped a tall can of beer he'd bought at Circle

K. He was having a nice night but that changed when Garrett slid into the driveway. Johnny liked silence—gawdammit—and dark desert nights and breezes that dried the sweat on his forehead. He liked cold beer and T-bones and boots that fit like they were born on his feet. He didn't like interruptions, shitty jokes, or foreign-made pickup trucks.

Garrett climbed out of the Sentra and ran a hand through his mop of red hair. He smacked a pack of cigarettes against his palm and looked at the sky. The stars were all spread out, hurtling laser-like toward the Earth. "Your sister here?"

"No smoking on our property." Johnny's lanky fingers squeezed dents into his beer can. He leaned forward, stood.

Garrett ignored him and lit a cigarette. "I just came by to see Lorrie, that's all."

"You gotta park so nobody else can squeeze in, that how you have to do it?"

Garrett looked back at his little car and surveyed the driveway. He shrugged. "You sad you don't have company?" A rusted aluminum rowboat was parked on the driveway's far side and Johnny's light orange pickup—a seventies step-side Ford—was parked up front, closer to the house. "Anybody else coming around, right now? I'm just picking Lorrie up. I'll be gone in a few short minutes. You mind having a little patience?" Garrett exhaled, blew some smoke through pursed lips and stepped toward the porch. "I'm not doing nothing."

"Don't you set foot on this porch." Johnny smacked at the window with the back of his hand. "Get the pistol." Johnny's little brother, Xavier—ten years old and wild as a jackrabbit—moved aside the curtains and

85

peered at him from behind the dirty window. "Get the pistol," Johnny repeated. The curtain swung shut and the kid disappeared somewhere inside the house, scampered off to hunt down the gun.

"We don't have to get like that." Garrett puffed on his cigarette some more. "Lorrie!" He planted his feet in the dirt and crossed his arms. "Lorrie!" Garrett spotted a few broken roof tiles sprinkled in the dirt near the porch. Next to the tiles were three white golf balls. "What happened with those?" He nodded at the mess and smirked. "New hobby?"

Johnny clenched his teeth and groaned. "Bastards next door came out and hit some golf balls at us. Pissed me off, too. Pulled out my .22 and took a few shots at them for fun. They're lucky I missed on purpose."

"Those jerk-offs over there?" Garrett lifted his chin toward the house in the distance. It was ringed by a chain-link fence and the windows near the front poured yellow light into the soft darkness. "Should have plugged one of them in the kneecap."

"They do it again," Johnny said, "and I will."

Lorrie came outside and slammed the front door behind her. She had black eyeliner and mascara on with a short skirt that made Johnny want to punch the side of a tree. "Hey," she said and grinned at Garrett. Her nineteen-year-old lips turned pouty and with one finger she brushed a long black curl out of her eyes. "I missed you today. You didn't call me this morning." She lifted her cell phone in one hand and waved it like a flag. "You didn't even text."

"You going out with him now, huh?" Johnny lifted his thick eyebrows and smacked his lips. Her damn skirt was too short for comfort. "I don't remember you saying anything about this punk."

"Johnny, be quiet. It's mine and Garrett's six-week anniversary."

"Six-week anniversary?" Johnny eyeballed Garrett and made note of the way the punk's lips pointed at his nose and how he bounced one knee up and down like a druggie. He was up to nothing good—Johnny could tell that just from the way he puffed on a cigarette. He got a bad feeling from Garrett, like the guy was plotting something.

Lorrie ran to Garrett's car, got in and slammed the passenger door. Johnny followed her off the porch and ambled over to the red-haired punk. The two men— Garrett, at twenty-two and some odd months, more boyish than Johnny, though they were close to the same age—put their faces right up against each other like angry, punch-drunk boxers. The cigarette dangled from Garrett's lips. Johnny reached up and pinched it between his thumb and index finger. He tossed it into the dirt and stomped. "I don't want to see you here anymore."

"You ain't tough, big bro."

"Maybe not, but I'm mean."

"Go easy on me," Garrett backed away a few steps. He turned around and walked to his car. "I'll take care of her."

The front door opened and Xavier ran outside, handed Johnny the pistol. His bare feet padded in the dirt, crunched into tiny fists as he stepped on prickly goat-heads. He stood behind his big brother and watched.

Garrett hopped into the Sentra and threw it in reverse. He backed out of the driveway. The Sentra rattled and sputtered, shot white smoke from the tailpipe.

Johnny planted his feet and fired the pistol once into the air. Then he picked up a rock and threw it as hard as he could at the dirty white car whose belts squealed like mice. "Punk bitch!"

Garrett spun out in the dirt and took off down the road. The rock smacked against his bumper but didn't do any damage.

Little Xavier laughed and said, "Hell yeah, bro."

Garrett bounced the Sentra over the highway's center median and screeched to a stop in the parking lot outside Old Miner's, the most popular bar in town. The place looked pretty full for a weeknight. A healthy smattering of pickup trucks and rundown beaters were parked in feigned ignorance of the dirt parking lot's chalk-white lines. "Here we are, paradise at last." Garrett shifted the car into park and pulled the keys from the ignition. "You gonna drink cosmopolitans or order a real drink tonight?"

In the passenger seat, Lorrie dabbed at her cheeks with one hand while she held a small compact mirror in the other. "I look old enough to you?"

"Shit, how am I supposed to answer that? I think you look all grown up, little lady." A sneaky grin grew on his face and he lit a cigarette. "You want one?" He lodged it in his mouth and puffed.

"I told you, it smells."

"So?"

"So, don't expect me to kiss you after you've been smoking."

"You sound like my grandma, dammit. We can smoke something else if you want. What do you say to that?"

Lorrie lifted an eyebrow at him, swung her gaze back to the mirror. "Doesn't your grandma smoke? I thought she did."

"Sure does. That doesn't mean she won't bitch at you. You know how it is."

"Yeah." Lorrie snapped the compact shut and shoved it into her leopard-print purse. "I think I'm ready."

"You think?" Garrett dragged from his cigarette and squinted at Lorrie through gray smoke. "You gotta know, baby. Either that or they're gonna know you're a little girl. You don't want that, do you?"

"Screw you, Garrett. Let's go." Lorrie swept a black curl behind her ear. "And don't call me 'baby.'"

Lorrie and Garrett squeezed onto bar stools in a far corner. Old Miner's was crowded and Lorrie started sweating right away. Rockabilly music poured from the jukebox in harsh flurries and the dance floor seemed lost beneath the thunderous clap of scuffed boots and cheap high heels. Lorrie leaned into Garrett's ear, brushed her wet lips against his neck. "This how it always is?"

Before Garrett could nod, a woman yelped along a back wall where two pool tables catered to a large group of barely-of-age locals. Three booths along the wall closest to the door were taken by older folks, some Lorrie recognized from around town. Brown beer bottles sat in groups in the center of every table. One guy Lorrie didn't know but had seen around town a lot lately. A biker who rode a Harley Davidson and never wore a shirt beneath his leather vest. Now he squinted at her from across the dance floor. He had a stark white beard, bushy beneath his wide chin, and cold blue eyes that made her shiver.

Garrett waved at the bartender before pressing his lips against Lorrie's ear. "It's busy for a Wednesday, but this is the cheapest drink in town. Beers are two for one today. Shit, that's better than the liquor store."

Lorrie twisted her face against his neck and said, "Get me one, why don't you? I'm thirsty." She wiped sweat from her forehead.

The bartender, an old guy named Ray, limped over and raised his eyebrows. Ray always wore a red flannel shirt and dirty Levis. He pulled small change from a wallet he kept lashed to his back pocket with a long silver chain. He carried a wood-handled hunting knife in a sheath along his right hip. Ray was known to come over the bar when it was necessary and talk was that he could handle himself, that he could throw a good, hard punch.

And Garrett knew from experience—the limp was just for show.

He slapped a ten-dollar bill on the bar. "Two beers and a shot of Beam." He leaned into Lorrie again and breathed a heavy sigh into her ear. "What's your brother got against me? Why's he gotta be such an asshole?"

"That's just how Johnny is. You come around more often and it'll be fine. Just make sure you bring beer. That makes his world go round."

"I can do that."

Ray popped the tops on two beers and slid a shot of Beam toward Garrett. He slapped a wrinkled five-dollar bill on the bar and limped away without eyeballing

Lorrie. Looked like he was going to let her do her thing.

Lorrie fingered a lock of hair and took a sip from her beer. So much for looking young. Maybe she was past her prime. She angled her eyes toward Garrett and laughed at him when he choked on his Jim Beam. "You're such a wimp, baby."

Garrett grinned and slid a hand along the small of her back. "First drink of the night, that's all. You offended he didn't ask for ID? Yeah, you're offended. I can tell."

"What the hell did I pay two hundred dollars for? A fake ID I never get to use?"

"Pretty much. That's how it is. You need it when you don't have it, and you never have it when it comes time you need it."

"Like money."

Garrett said, "That's right. Just like money."

Little Xavier liked to sit in the dark.

Ever since his daddy took that long trip up north, Xavier stopped using his bedroom lamp. He knew where everything was anyhow—why use the light? He used to read Spiderman comic books, but now all he did was shuffle a deck of cards over and over again. Or, like tonight, he twirled his daddy's pistol in one hand like a gunfighter. The pistol spun in slow revolutions along the middle knuckle of his index finger.

What Xavier wanted to do was this: he wanted to get so he could scare the shit out of his big brother.

Scare the shit out of Johnny, now that would be funny.

He wanted to walk out into the living room with the

pistol in his waistband, pull it out, and twirl it like Doc Holliday. Maybe he'd point the sucker at Johnny and shoot a hole in the wall next to his head. Yeah, that would be some funny shit. He couldn't wait to do it. First, though, he needed to get the spin so he could do it without looking at the pistol. He was almost there.

Xavier knew his big brother didn't tell him everything about Daddy's long trip—it pissed him off and he didn't know why.

Lorrie either. She kept saying to go ask Johnny.

Johnny told him to get a life and read a book. Asshole.

But Daddy was gone and Xavier couldn't figure out what happened. Only thing he knew was he didn't have anybody to play with, and the Sunday hamburgers weren't as good because Johnny didn't know what the hell he was doing. Xavier liked hamburgers, but not when they were burned and tasted like firewood. He missed his daddy. And now he played alone in the dark.

Xavier twirled the pistol, stopped it with his thumb and lodged it inside his too-large skater shorts. He drummed his fingers on the dresser. Thoughts bounced through his head. He didn't know what to do. He was bored, but he knew Johnny would tell him it was only boring people who got bored. Xavier sat cross-legged on the floor, picked up his pack of blue-backed playing cards, and began to shuffle.

A trick his daddy taught him, two thumbs to riffle the cards into two piles and a reverse bridge into one stack—from there you fire the cards like ninja stars. That's what Xavier did, fired the cards like ninja stars across the room.

They smacked the far wall and landed in a pile.

* * *

Lorrie spotted the guy as she stumbled from the women's bathroom. Not two hours into the night and she was drunk. He leaned against the wall near where the hallway opened like a mouth into the bar, one hand shoved into the front pocket of his tight-fitting Levis. His white beard poured from his chin like sea foam. That rockabilly music still banged from the speakers and all Lorrie wanted was some peace and quiet. If only for a minute or two. She pushed her way out the emergency exit and fell into the cool night air.

He followed her into the night. The door swung shut behind him and the muffled music sounded like a delivery man knocking at an apartment door.

"You come out here to pick me up?"

"You're a little young, don't you think?"

"I'm all grown up." Lorrie leaned against the wall and pulled a cigarette from her tiny purse. Hell, now she was smoking. All it took was a couple of beers.

"No, you're not." The biker pulled a lighter from inside his leather vest, lit it and touched the flame to her cigarette. "I think you're still a kid."

"You gonna turn me in or something?" She puffed, exhaled.

He shook his head.

"What then?"

"Who's the tough guy with you, the red-haired guy?"

"My fucking boyfriend. Who do you think?"

"He's bad news." The guy ran thick fingers through his beard, bore his blue eyes into her. "I just came outside to tell you."

"Why? Because he sells a little pot?"

"That all it is?"

"I don't know. Who cares?"

"You should. A guy like that, sometimes he winds up in a bad situation."

Lorrie coughed, tried to keep her eyes wide. The drinks were getting to her and she felt sleepy. She pushed against the wall, stood straighter. "What do you care?"

The guy shifted his boots in the dirt, looked toward the parking lot. A light breeze tossed dust about the pickup trucks, scattered dried creosote branches beneath tires and rusted, off-kilter truck bodies. Along the highway, a few pairs of headlights swept past, drained into the distance with blinking red taillights. "Maybe I don't. Still, I see a girl wander in with some lowlife punk, but the girl, she's alright. It's the guy who's the trouble. So, I think to myself I got to show her what's what—so she doesn't get hurt."

"Let me guess." She paused and squinted at him through a cloud of smoke. "You were up north with my daddy, am I right?"

"Never been up north, not me."

"You know him somehow."

The guy shrugged. His lips twitched. "You going to listen to me?"

Lorrie laughed. Her voice came out high-pitched, like someone pulled her hair. "Nope, I don't think I will." It sounded final.

The guy turned and sauntered toward the parking lot.

Lorrie watched him for a moment and said, "You never told me your name. Who are you?"

Over his shoulder, the guy said, "I was your guardian angel, but not anymore."

Lorrie propped her head against the wall and puffed until the cigarette was done. She tossed it into the dirt and crushed it with the bottom of a high heel shoe. She looked after the guy, but he'd disappeared around the corner.

Lorrie thought about his cold blue eyes.

She shivered.

Rex lay in bed, sheets bunched at his feet, and stared at the ceiling. He lifted a hand, flexed it. Tremors of pain ran from his fingers into his wrist. Damn, it hurt. For Rex, it got so his fingers bled and his muscles quivered—his tendons and ligaments like guitar strings ran taut from elbow to shoulder. He dropped his hand and lodged it behind his head.

Maybe he needed a new pillow. Or a new job.

Shit, maybe Rex needed a new life.

When he started the job—stocking lumber and sheet rock at a local hardware store—Rex carried ten pounds of beer fat on his gut. Too many parties out in the sticks while he finished high school. My, how that fat drained off his wiry frame. Three months of work and Rex found himself hungry no matter what he ate. Lickety-split, like that. Shit, he could drink a six pack every night and not gain any weight, that is if he managed to stay up past nine or ten.

Rex found himself dead-tired after work. Tired as a damn dog.

Each day it was the same: He got there at seven and helped unload any new deliveries. They used a forklift when they could, but the place was old and had some tight spaces. Sometimes that meant moving things by hand, one piece at a time. The guys Rex worked with, they laughed at him. Shit, he knew it wasn't the hardest work—it wasn't digging ditches or laying asphalt under the desert sun.

No, Rex had it easy.

But if this was easy, and if it was all he'd ever be—man, Rex wasn't good with that.

Not a chance.

It pissed him off, made him grit his teeth and toss two-by-fours across the lumber yard until the other guys laughed at him through their yellow teeth and cigarette smoke. "You alright over there, Rex?"

He grunted and looked through them with fiery eyes. "I'm fine, just getting some shit done."

Yes—he took pride in the work, but it didn't change the fact that his body ached and his mind fell dormant and his days shrank before his eyes. *The way it is son*, that's what his daddy used to say. *The way it is and the way it always will be.* And Rex believed that. He believed it with every beat of his heart. Still, it pissed him off. Day after day at the hardware store. A few dollars every other week and that's about it. Every day when Rex woke up he said to himself, *Get to work, pal. If you don't hurry, you're gonna be late. Wake up and get to work.* Maybe this was why he couldn't sleep. Rex didn't want to wake up in the morning. Not tomorrow. Not the next day.

Shit, not ever.

It was over lunch that Ralph mentioned it to Rex. "You ever need some weed," he said, "my guy'll do you right. Specials on weekends and holidays, too."

Rex took a bite from an apple, chewed. "I'm good. Don't really smoke too much."

"Just saying, Garrett'll get you what you need—if you ever need anything. All you do is tell me and I'll hook you up." Ralph rapped his knuckles against the table in the break room, spoke through his teeth like the thing was a secret. "I'm telling you for real, now. You need a deal, I can get you one."

Rex chewed some more, took another bite. "What makes you think I want weed, Ralph? I look like a stoner to you?" Ralph was in his early fifties, but he looked like seventy, talked like it too. Rex didn't think he'd make it long in the job. The man had only been hired part-time, and he worked like shit—showed up late most days. "Anyway, who the hell is Garrett?"

"My dealer, man. He's my guy."

"Your dealer?"

"My guy. He's my guy." Ralph said the short sentence like it was a long one. He rapped his knuckles on the table again.

"I'll let you know."

Ralph nodded, stood, and walked out of the break room into the hall. Rex could hear him whistle while he walked, oblivious. Across the break room, one of the cashiers peered up at Rex from a magazine, raised his eyebrows, and shrugged. The cashier looked back down, took another bite of potato salad.

Rex plunged his teeth into the apple, chewed.

It sounded like a sales pitch—a shot in the dark—and that's exactly what it was, but Rex saw Ralph saunter over to a mud-flecked, blue Sentra in the parking lot after work. Rex watched from the driver's seat of his Toyota as Ralph bobbed his head at the Sentra's driver then climbed into the passenger seat. The two men exchanged merchandise in less than thirty seconds—Ralph slammed the Sentra's door and walked over to his pickup truck, got it started and drove out onto the highway. The guy in the blue Sentra, he sat there for a while, looked down into his lap and counted his money. After a few minutes, he rolled out of the parking lot. White smoke poured from the tailpipe and gangster rap rattled through the windows.

Rex recognized the car. He'd seen it parked out front of Johnny's pad, most times late at night. The guy driving though, Rex didn't know him, had never seen him before this evening. Rex committed the fucker's face to memory—a squirrel-fur goatee and close-set eyes over a knife-edge nose. A diamond earring glared from his left lobe. He wore a gold chain around his neck, too. So, this was Ralph's boy, Garrett.

Rex wondered how much weed Garrett carried on him, how he made the rounds to all his customers, kept the town supplied. Not like Rex would know what to do with it. Nope, he'd have a hard time giving it to people. But who was this guy, Garrett? A friend of Johnny's? Lorrie's boyfriend? Maybe, that was probably it.

The thought of Garrett chilling over at Johnny's, his lips pressed against Lorrie's while the car sat outside unattended, crossed Rex's mind. He sat in the cab and thought for a few minutes. His arms felt rubbery from the long day at work and he didn't feel like lifting them to steer the truck.

Man, he didn't know how people did it day after day for fifty damn years. That shit just seemed impossible to him. Rex looked toward his dim future as if through binoculars. He saw himself from a distant remove.

There he was struggling to climb out of bed in the early mornings, and there he was still lurching across the lumber yard like a damn zombie. It was a feeling that came over him from time to time. The future was the same as right now, and that's all it'd ever be, a repeat of the now. Rex dragged his gaze through the darkening air and set his eyes on the empty parking space, the spot where the Sentra had parked.

That motherfucker right there, just slinging weed and staying up late. Not a damn care in the world. It just doesn't seem fair, now does it?

Rex sucked air through his teeth.

He tapped his keys into his palm and glarcd across the parking lot.

Man, he sure needed a drink.

Johnny powered his Ford step-side through a final curve before topping Canyon Crest. He squinted into the fading sunlight that splashed upwards from the horizon. Up ahead on the roadside was a blue car flecked with mud hoisted by a portable lift—one of those cheap jacks from Walmart. He flipped off his radio—country was sounding less and less like country anyway—and ignited his hazard lights.

It looked like Garrett's car.

He pulled to the shoulder, grimaced as the gravel rattled against his truck's body, and put the sucker in park. It was Garrett alright. Johnny climbed out and walked toward the car.

Garrett knelt near the driver's side front tire. His cheeks were red and sweat slicked the back of his neck.

Johnny stopped, lodged his hands on his hips. "What

the hell is it, Garrett?" He looked off toward the sunset, registered the light fading behind flat, cacti-spiked expanse, and turned his eyes back to the kid on his knees.

Johnny sniffed, exhaled dust.

A few pickup trucks rattled past them on the high-way. A motorcycle thundered from somewhere below and a Harley Davidson crested the hill. The white-bearded rider lifted a hand to them as he roared through the dusk.

Garrett labored to his feet and shook his head. Black grease shaded his forehead and right cheek. In his hands, he held a cheap, chrome crossbar tire iron. Again, it was the kind they sold at the Walmart in town. "Flat tire," he said. "Son-of-a-bitch won't come loose though. I don't know what the hell." As Johnny came around to take a look, Garrett knelt again and put all his weight into turning one of the lug nuts. It didn't budge.

Johnny laughed and slipped his thumbs through his belt loops. "You need a breaker-bar, that's all. Not enough leverage like that."

"What's that?"

This sucker doesn't even know what a breaker-bar is. Shit. "Hand me that jack handle. Let me show you what to do. Nobody ever taught you to change a tire?"

"I know how to change it. It just won't come off, that's all." Garrett handed Johnny a blue jack handle and stood. "Take a shot. I hope you do better than me."

"Watch out." Johnny bent to one knee, positioned the tire iron so one end pointed at the sky, and slipped the hollow jack handle over the tire iron. He tilted the whole assembly forward and the lug turned, no prob-lem. "See that?"

"Damn—thanks a lot. A breaker-bar. I like that."

Johnny stood and wiped his hands across his pants. "You can do the rest yourself. You heading up to the house?"

"I was thinking about it. Thought I might miss you, but here we are."

"Yeah, well, I got off early today." Johnny scratched his chin. He guessed the kid wasn't so bad. Maybe he should let up on him a little bit. "You working these days?"

"Look, I should be honest." Garrett looked down at the breaker-bar. It hung askew, angled across the flat tire. "I do alright, but I sell pot. That's my gig—I don't get into that hard stuff. The way I see it, pot's like medicine. Most of the people I sell to, I guess you could say they're my patients." Garrett met Johnny's eyes.

It sounded stupid when he said it aloud, but Johnny could tell from the way Garrett set his mouth that he meant it. "My sister's dating a pot dealer, that what you're saying?"

"I guess so."

"Well, look at us—regular old white trash. Am I right?"

"I wouldn't say trash."

"Nope," Johnny said, "me neither." He studied Garrett's grease-stained face. "A man needs to work and make money. I know that. Shit, how he does it, that's up to him."

"I appreciate you saying it."

"I guess you know about my dad, huh?"

"I heard."

Johnny nodded, sniffed more dust and sneezed once, wiped his nose with the back of his hand. "There's a baseball game on tonight. I'll see you up at the house."

"I'll bring beer," Garrett said.

Johnny ambled back to his truck, climbed inside and started it. He revved the engine and accelerated onto the highway. His headlights swam toward the flat horizon, two bright pinpricks burning into darkness.

Up at Johnny's house, Garrett took care to park his blue Sentra next to the old boat. He lined everything up right so it looked uniform, like the driveway was a paved lot or something.

He was getting on Johnny's good side, better not mess that up.

He yanked a case of beer from the trunk—a Circle K special on account of Fourth of July coming up that weekend—and stepped onto the porch. Before he could knock, Johnny's little brother opened the door and flipped Garrett off with a tiny middle finger. "The fuck you doing here again?" The kid lifted his other hand and mirrored the gesture.

"Shit," Garrett said. "You got some manners—I can dig that."

Johnny's voice came from inside the house. "Let him in, Xavier. He's bringing us some beer. At least that's what he said."

"Damn well better," Xavier let the door swing open and walked down the hall. A bedroom door slammed and he disappeared.

Garrett entered and plopped himself on the couch. He ripped open the case of beer and popped a can, sipped from it. On the television—it was a decent-sized flat screen—the Dodgers warmed up on the field. They were playing the Padres down in San Diego. Garrett called toward the kitchen, "You a Dodgers fan?"

Johnny came in and sat down in a beige recliner that reminded Garrett of a giant pillow. He kicked the chair back and stuck his boots into the air. "Toss me one." Garrett tossed him a beer. Johnny popped the top and guzzled for a good ten seconds. "Ah. I like the Dodgers, but the sons-of-bitches drive me nuts. Last year they got this slugger from over there in Cuba—paid a shit-ton for this guy. All he does is make throwing errors from center. It's ridiculous. Better off bringing a kid up from the farm system. Got your tire changed, huh?"

"Yeah. I changed it no problem. Thanks for the help, man." Garrett paused for a second and added, "I saw one of your high school games a couple years ago. I remember you stole home. Fucking ballsy is what it was. Slid head first, too."

A faint laugh floated from between Johnny's lips. He nodded his head and pressed his mouth into a look of disappointment. "I wasn't too bad a player. Never did anything with it though. I remember that game, first time in twenty years someone stole home in a league game. I got laid after that."

"A double steal," Garrett said.

"Shit."

Down the hall, a bedroom door opened and Lorrie came into the living room. She wore a short black skirt and Doc Marten boots that ran to just below her knees. "What the hell?" She lifted her palms toward the ceiling. "You're not even gonna say hello? You come to see him or to see me? He doesn't even like you."

Garrett coughed once and sat straighter on the couch. He swallowed another sip of beer. "We're hanging out, that's all." He ran a hand through his red hair. "You got a problem with me and Johnny hanging out, or what?"

"Damn, looks like somebody's whipped," Johnny said.

"Shut up, Johnny." Lorrie stomped across the thin carpet and grabbed Garrett's hand. "Let's go to my room. You don't want to hang out with this clown."

Garrett looked over at Johnny, waited for a response.

Johnny waved a hand and set his eyes on the baseball game. "She's your problem now, pal. Get thee gone and out of my face."

Lorrie dragged Garrett out of the living room and down the hallway.

From the living room, Johnny's voice floated after them like a bird: "That skirt is too damn short."

"Fuck you," Lorrie said over her shoulder. "I can wear what I want."

The bedroom door slammed.

Rex felt a little better after a drink at Old Miner's. He cracked a window as he piloted the Toyota through the curves on Canyon Crest. Warm air hit his lips and cheeks, made his eyes widen. The memory of Garrett selling weed to Ralph faded in his head, drifted behind a fog that made it seem a dream.

Maybe things weren't so bad.

Shit, he had a job—that was something.

Rex sang along to an AC/DC song on the radio and thought about a girl named Gladis he saw down at the bar. She had a sweet voice and nice, pouty lips. He caught her eyeballing him but didn't make a move. He promised himself, next time I'm going to ask her for a dance. If it's the last thing I do. Rex steered the Toyota onto his street, bit the inside of his cheek and rolled up the window. As he turned toward home, he caught a slight flash against the perimeter of his high beams—the blue Sentra. He stopped the Toyota and smirked. Gladis disappeared from his head as if his thoughts were a man walking into a mirage. First, she was there. And then, she was gone. Garrett surfaced. "There you are, you fuck."

Rex flipped on his fog lights and rolled past Johnny's house.

Since the night with the golf balls, Johnny had come out and fired warning shots each night over Rex and Lou's place. It wasn't exactly comfortable living. At first, it was funny. But Rex got nervous when the shots started tearing apart the Joshua tree out back and plinking against the steel pylons that held the chain-link fence upright. Turned out Johnny was one hell of a shot with his rifle. Rex contemplated calling the cops—shit, Lou even suggested it—but that would make them soft, and it'd make them snitches to boot. One thing about living out in the middle of the desert, you only called the authorities as a last resort.

As he drove past the house, Rex saw the quick flash of the flat-screen television and a bedroom light in one of the side windows. Looked like Lorrie was home. He registered, again, the blue Sentra out front—mud flecked and missing a hubcap.

Yep, it was Garrett, the pot dealer.

Well, fuck me.

* * *

"Another day in the life," Lou said. His boots rested on the uneven coffee table and a beer cooled his hand. He reclined on the pleather couch, a slight smirk draped along the bottom of his face. "Any good shit happen at work?"

Rex got himself a beer and sat on the carpet. "Nope, same old shit. What about you?"

"Same shit. Some chick brought in her Honda Civic. Get this. It's a 2010 model. Not too old, right? She's never changed the oil. Never even checked it. I says to her, 'When's the last time you had the oil changed?' She gives me a look like I'm fucking crazy, a look like this." Lou curled his mouth and opened his eyes wide.

"You're kidding me." Rex slammed back his beer, drained the bottle.

"Crazy thing is, it's still running like a beast. She brought it in because she heard the brakes squeaking. Fucking-A. That's a good car, that Honda. If only America could make a car like that and ship the fucker overseas."

"I doubt people would buy an American car overseas."

"Fuck you, Rex. You terrorist."

They both laughed and Rex walked into the kitchen for a couple new bottles. "You ever see that blue Sentra over at Johnny's?" He pulled two bottles from the fridge, handed one to Lou and sat down again. "It's there right now."

"Yeah—it's been there quite a bit lately. Why?"

"Guy deals pot, I'm pretty sure. Ralph, one of the stoners at work, told me that the guy, Garrett, will hook it up whenever I want."

"I thought you didn't smoke weed." Lou pressed the cold beer bottle against his forehead. "You feel like it's time to let loose, huh?"

"Not exactly. See, what I was thinking was that the car probably isn't locked—I mean, it might not be, right?"

"So?"

"So, how'd it be to come up on a bunch of pot and sell it?"

Lou grunted and breathed hard through his nose. "You, a pot dealer? I doubt you could pull that off, Rex. Come on, man—it's not a good idea. It's a horrible idea."

"Fuck you, it's not. All we need to do is go get it. We just sell that shit over a few months. It's extra cash. Besides, that's not the point. This fucker doesn't even work. He lives down fucking easy street."

"The play isn't to steal his pot then, it's to hit him up for the fucking money he makes. We're going to make money, we need to take it from him." Lou sipped from his beer and smiled. "You see what I'm saying? I mean, if you were going to do it, that is."

Rex thought for a moment. It made sense. Fuck the pot, it was the money he wanted. He nodded and drained the second beer. "You're right. It's the money. We'd need to take him for his money. So," Rex said, "if you were going to do it, how would it go down?"

"You ever gonna get a real job, baby?" Lorrie lifted Garrett's hand from her bare stomach. She turned over and stared at the black-and-white picture on her nightstand; her and Johnny and Xavier standing next to daddy outside the house. Daddy wore a Dodgers cap twisted sideways on his head and a gap-toothed smile. Lorrie's lanky arms draped around his waist. Her fingernails pressed into the firm bone of his hip. This picture was taken a few weeks before Daddy made the long trip up to Lompoc State Prison. It was a trip he wouldn't come back from and pretty much everybody knew it. Though Johnny decided not to tell Xavier—he kept putting it off until Xavier stopped asking.

Yet another thing her family did wrong, at odds with convention.

She hated that. Maybe she could change it. "It's important to me," Lorrie said, "that we do things the right way."

Garrett coughed three times before lighting a cigarette. He puffed a little and coughed again. "These fuckers are killing me."

"Like I've been telling you."

"Selling weed, Lorrie—that's my job. It pays damn good, too. Pretty soon I'll have enough saved up for a place out here, maybe one of these repo joints, one of the tract homes on two acres. You'd like that, right? I mean, who else is gonna give you that? I'm talking about a place of our own, me and you."

"I want a family though. I want some kids and two cars and dinner parties."

"Dinner parties?"

"You know what I mean."

"You don't even cook."

"I bake cookies, don't I?"

"But what about the dinner?"

"You know what I mean."

Garrett shrugged and tapped ash onto the thin carpet. He stared at the night sky through an open bedroom window. "I get it, and I'm trying. I just need you to give me a few more months. We'll get our own place. I promise you that, but you gotta run it by Johnny. Last thing I need is your brother on my ass. He still don't like me."

"Johnny will be fine. What about a job?"

"I have one."

"Nope, I mean for real—like Johnny."

Garrett ran his hand along Lorrie's bare hip. She shrugged him off and scooted out of reach. He dragged from the cigarette and blew a gray smoke ring. With a long-nailed finger, Garrett scratched his chin. "What kind of job you think I could do?"

"Anything. Work for the water company, telephone company. You could go down and work with Johnny at the truck dealership."

"And do what?"

"Whatever he does."

Garrett shook his head. He set the cigarette down on the nightstand nearest him and leaned toward Lorrie. He dragged a finger across her knee, onto the smooth plain of her thigh. "I already got a job," he said. "I'm clocked in right now."

Lorrie giggled. She took another look at the picture of Daddy and her brothers and herself. She liked this guy, this pot dealer named Garrett. She really did.

Lorrie turned and caught his lips with her own.

Johnny watched six innings, but middle relief blew the game for the Dodgers and he got pissed. Fuckers. He flipped off the flat screen and wandered into the kitchen. His kid brother never did dishes, so Johnny washed a few plates plastered with peanut butter and jelly. He felt bad about leaving the kid alone after school, but Johnny worked till six or seven most days—Xavier would have to make do until, well, until forever.

Johnny cursed his dad. "Asshole. Dumb fuck." Got himself locked up and wouldn't be coming back, not anytime soon. He turned off the faucet and stared out the window. The desert stretched itself out behind the house and seemed to wave beneath the darkness. A light wind tossed the brush back and forth, made the Joshua trees shiver. "Fuck, man."

"Who you talking to?"

Johnny turned around and smiled at his little brother. "Hey, pal. What you up to?"

"Nothing. Can I watch a movie since baseball's over?"

"Shit. The game isn't over, it's just—yeah, actually it's over. Go ahead, but don't sit too close to the TV."

"We need more peanut butter, Johnny."

"I know, pal. I'll pick up some groceries tomorrow. School going good, or what?"

"It's alright, I started playing soccer during recess."

"Soccer? Shit, what the hell for?"

"It's fun, Johnny. I scored some goals."

Johnny studied his kid brother, looked for that faint trace of sadness in the kid's eyes. It came after Daddy went north, but man had it lingered. Right now, Johnny couldn't see it, but he knew it was there. Johnny worried about Xavier, tried to be some kind of father figure, but he knew Xavier didn't see him like that. "That's good, X—hell, yes. What about spelling, you good with that?"

"We had to spell transportation."

"Spell it for me."

"Well, I got it wrong."

"Shit."

"That's what I said."

Johnny grinned. "You better not have, not at school."

Xavier shook his head, lifted his eyebrows. "Shit."

"Shit," Johnny said.

"Balls and shit."

"Alright, that's enough." Johnny laughed. "You watch whatever you want, pal."

Xavier smiled at his big brother, a kind of half-smile that lit and faded like a matchstick aflame. He drifted into the living room, flipped on the flat screen, and dove into the couch.

In the kitchen, Johnny watched the lights from the flat screen flash against darkness. Maybe Xavier would make it through all this. But then again, maybe not. Maybe none of them would make it through this. Johnny crossed his arms. *I know. Shit, I'm gonna get me another beer and take a few shots at those suckers up the street.* He opened the door that joined the garage to the kitchen, walked through it to get his rifle.

"The fuck is he shooting at now?"

Lorrie rolled her eyes, lifted the blanket to her neck and pressed a bare thigh against Garrett's flank. "Those guys next door. Johnny's still pissed about them hitting golf balls at our place. For the last few days he's been out there, shooting holes in their stucco. It's ridiculous—something Daddy would do."

"Oh, right. Are they just little punks, or what?"

"No," Lorrie said, "our age. Like everybody in this town, they like to cause trouble. Think it's funny, I guess."

"Should I go out there?"

"No way. Let Johnny have his fun. He's just fucking

around. Besides, the last thing you need is to have Rex and Lou as enemies."

"Why's that? You don't think I can hold my own?"

"I do. It's just that...Rex, well, he acts kind of hard," Lorrie said. "I've never seen him fight, but I bet he's taken guys bigger than you down before."

Garrett lifted the blanket. "Bigger than that?"

Lorrie giggled. "Alright, Mr. Hard-ass—whatever you say."

"You sure I shouldn't go out there, help Johnny?"

Another shot rang through the music on the radio. Lorrie shook her head and exhaled. "I think he's got it. Let him blow off some steam."

"You're mad at your dad still, I take it."

"Wouldn't you be?" Lorrie moved away from him, closed her eyes. "You think I should pat him on the back, or what?"

"What would you do if I got caught?"

Lorrie's eyes opened. "You better not."

"I won't, but it's possible. I mean, fuck, I could get caught."

Lorrie shook her head, folded her bottom lip beneath a row of teeth. "I swear," she said.

"Hey, I'm kidding. I brought it up as a joke." Garrett ran a finger along her cheek. "I'm kidding, alright?" Another rifle shot sounded, died amid a brief shattering sound. "I think he got a window."

Voices echoed in the distance. Johnny shouted back a response. Sounded like a curse.

"God," Lorrie said. "I feel like I live in the Wild West or something. What the fuck?" She burned her eyes into Garrett's. "Do me a favor, don't get fucking caught, understand?"

Garrett met her gaze and grinned. One cheek dimpled and he rested his head on a shoulder, ruffled his stark red hair with a hand. "Ain't nobody getting caught," he said. "Not in my operation they're not."

The next morning, before the sun crested incisor peaks along the horizon's edge, Rex swung his Toyota through a blinking yellow stoplight, slammed on the brakes, and pulled into Dave's Liquor Store. He needed to pick up lunch for his shift, maybe an energy drink or two. Rex felt like he lived on energy drinks, like maybe his blood would freeze up, coagulate in his veins if he stopped drinking a couple each day. Today might be a three energy-drink day.

See if that stopped his heart.

Him and Lou didn't get the best sleep after dodging rifle rounds. Now Rex needed to pick up a new window for the living room. Johnny shattered the fucker—that sharp-eyed bastard. Rex knew that this whole feud, somehow, would come to an end. Who might get the best of it, Rex didn't know.

Johnny meant business, that's what all those rifle rounds were saying.

Rex parked right out front of Dave's, looked up to see the square rectangle of light pouring from behind the large glass windows. It was more than a liquor store when you thought about it. Dave sold a little bit of every-thing for folks who got off work and didn't want to stop elsewhere. You could swing by in the evenings and see anybody you wanted—hell, they all needed beer, didn't they?

Beer, yes. And toothpaste and toilet paper and those

little packs of licorice, too. Rex switched off the ignition and reached for his wallet on the dashboard. As he looked up from the dash and into the wash of light from the storefront, Rex saw a ghost, an apparition, full-length and back from the dead. His father, a bent six feet with scarecrow shoulders draped in a Mexican serape, ambled toward the window. The old man—had to be around sixty years old now—scanned the aisle, left to right and right to left. He looked—in the hard features of his face—just like the man in the polaroid Rex found a few months back in his mom's storage unit. In scrawled cursive on the back of the photo she had written, "Dad, Xmas 1981." In the image, his father wore a black T-shirt and grease-stained Levis. Across his waist was a large, silver belt buckle in the shape of an electric guitar. His eyes were closed, but he was smiling. Rex knew the man looked just like him. Or, he looked just like the man. No question who fathered Rex. Both men had the same scrawny chest, the same turtle-like eyelids and, most similar, they both had hawk-talon noses. No telling what else the two of them shared. Rex hated to think it, but he suspected he was a lot like his father, that they were two men walking around in different bodies, their fortunes dead-set on the same sad prize—the prize of nothing.

He remembered what his dad used to say, *The way it is son, the way it is and the way it always will be.* For work, sure. But maybe for life, too.

Rex thought his father looked happy in the picture.

But Rex also thought the man looked drunk.

Happy? Maybe.

Drunk? You betcha.

Rex watched through the liquor store window as his father neared the end of the aisle. The man poked his head over the top shelf and scanned the store. The only clerk on duty was busy elsewhere. Rex's father reached down and pulled a bottle from a shelf. He lifted it to eye level and grinned. It was a clear bottle with blue-green liquid and before Rex could understand what his father was doing, the man violently twisted off the lid and drank it in one thirsty, vile motion. Blue-green liquid ran over his lips, dribbled down his chin and stained the front of his serape like it was a child's bib. There was an animal spirit about Rex's father, a half-man wildness that poured from his eyes.

Oh my.

His father, the man he hadn't heard from in two years—even after trying phone listings and prison records in three states—was drinking mouthwash like a fiend in Dave's Liquor Store. You go through all that trouble, look everywhere you can think to look, and you find the man right here in town. Rex's father swallowed the entire bottle in two long swigs and replaced the lid. He set the bottle back on the shelf and used a corner of his serape to dab at his mouth, a final gesture that struck Rex as both well-mannered and arrogant. "Jesus." That was all Rex could say as he watched the old man slink across the store and make a quick exit through the swinging glass doors. Rex's fingers wrapped around his door handle. He tensed them, started to pull, but he decided against it. Nope. Let the man go to wherever he's headed—no need to start a conversation that won't end.

Where you been?

A little bit of everywhere.

Didn't think to call?

What the hell for?

So we know where you been.

What do you care?

Rex spoke aloud to himself once more, "You son-of-a-bitch. You ghostly son-of-a-bitch. I never thought I'd see you again." Rex squinted and watched as his father moved off down the sidewalk; a lone, slim silhouette stumbling toward sunrise, a drunk in a serape going who knew where and killing time until who knew when.

The morning clerk, Sandoval, an old man with sleep-caked eyes and a patchy mustache, appeared from the store room as Rex entered the liquor store. Sandoval nodded at Rex and moved behind the counter, lifted a book of crossword puzzles, not wise at all to the mouth-wash he'd lost.

Behind the counter, Rex spotted a small television broadcasting a closed-circuit feed of the store. He saw himself on the screen, a slim character with a gray hooded sweater and work boots beneath frayed jeans. Well, he couldn't see that his jeans were frayed, not on the screen, but looking down he knew it as fact. The work boots were scuffed and spotted with white paint and mud. "Sandoval, how goes it?"

The old man looked at Rex, squinted. "I worked all night. I'm tired." He looked back at the book.

Rex wandered through the aisles. He picked up a package of sunflower seeds, energy drinks, a candy bar, and one of those soggy sub sandwiches packed with lettuce. He sauntered to the counter and dumped everything in front of Sandoval.

"Lunch, eh?" Sandoval shut the book, put it down on the counter. "Healthy eating for you. I like this kind," he said and lifted one of the energy drinks.

"You seen that guy before, Sandoval?"

"What guy?" He set down the drink, scanned the items with a little digital gun. "You mean the old man?"

Rex nodded. "The guy who was just in here."

"He comes in all the time. Every day. Never buys nothing, though. Maybe sometimes, but not today." He finished scanning and punched a button on the register. "Smells bad."

"How long he been coming here?"

Sandoval ran his eyes across the ceiling, twisted a corner of his mouth. "Like, one year at least. I can remember at least that long." He shook a paper sack from beneath the counter and stacked Rex's items inside it.

Rex heaved breath across the counter. "A fucking year?"

Sandoval said, "At least, maybe even longer. Why you care?"

"I've never seen him here."

"So, lots of people come in the store."

Rex shook his head and bit the inside of his cheek. "I can't believe it. You see what he did?" He pointed at the screen behind Sandoval, raised his eyebrows at the man. "Tell me you know he's a drunk."

"I know, but what did he do?"

Rex left the counter, found the aisle with the empty bottle of mouth wash. He brought it back to the counter and handed it to Sandoval. "See that?"

Sandoval looked at the bottle with great wonder. "Why?"

Rex tapped the counter with a finger. "There's alcohol inside, man. What do you think? He drank it, the whole fucking thing."

117

Sandoval said, "A thief. I knew it."

"Yeah, right."

"First, I get a robbing. Now another thief."

Rex handed him a ten-dollar bill and waited for the change. "Got robbed, huh? When that happen?"

Sandoval slid a few coins from the register and dumped them in Rex's hand. "Two nights ago. A big mean sucker." He leaned over the counter and tapped a small hole in the wood panel along its front. "Shot at me right here with his pistol."

Rex leaned down and, sure as shit, it was a bullet hole.

"Only seventy-five dollars for him. But a bullet coming at me—why?"

"Money, Sandoval. Is there another reason?" It was obvious to Rex.

The old man shook his head, batted his big, sleepy eyes.

"You get it on tape?"

Sandoval lifted a finger. "Yes. A tall man on a motorcycle. A white beard, like Santa Claus."

"No shit."

"None. A robbing by Santa Claus."

"Well, even Santa needs a few bucks. Never did picture him with a pistol though." Rex lifted his paper bag, clutched it to his chest. He walked toward the door but turned to Sandoval one last time. The man already had the crossword book close to his face. Rex said, "You see that old man, tell him his son is looking for him, alright?"

Sandoval looked at Rex, watched him push his way outside. He shook his head and grunted.

* * *

Saturday, mid-afternoon, and Lou was already drunk.

Rex shook his head and sipped from his own drink. *That boy can't handle his hard liquor.* They'd been drinking at Old Miner's since noon. A rockabilly band rattled off tunes in one corner and all the girls got over to the dance floor. The band's name was Sugar Tits and the lead singer kept saying so after every song. "We're Sugar Tits," he said, "and we got a new album came out last week. Five bucks and you can add it to your bar tab." Best Rex could tell, they played a whole bunch of Chuck Berry covers and a few Dylan songs all up tempo—he didn't hear anything original.

"Rex," Lou said. "You're paying today. I paid last week and you owe me."

"I don't owe you shit."

The pretty girl Rex had a thing for, Gladis, sauntered over to the bar and started talking his ear off about how good her hair salon business was doing. She was making rent in the strip mall off the highway and she even took out some ads in the local paper. Rex said he was proud of her and knew business would keep on going just like she hoped. He believed what he said. It was good to hear about a dream coming true.

"Thanks, Rex," Gladis said. "I want you to dance with me."

They walked onto the dance floor and Gladis pinned her midsection to Rex's hips and grabbed his ass. He sure as shit didn't mind. Her hair was pulled up into a high ponytail and Rex placed his palm on the back of her neck. Her skin was smooth and sweaty. They danced for a couple songs and kissed on the lips at the end. He felt good, like things might happen with Gladis, like she thought of him as more than he was, as a man. He hadn't expected it, but sometimes low expectations meant the good felt great. She pulled herself from him and drifted toward her giggling group of girlfriends.

Rex headed back for the bar.

That's when Garrett and Johnny walked into Old Miner's.

They both wore baseball caps pulled low over their eyes and Rex could tell Johnny was high. As far as Rex knew, Johnny wasn't into weed, but hanging with Garrett made getting high simple.

Lorrie walked in behind them. She dressed like she was going to a punk concert out in LA. This fact bothered people in town, including her own brother, but nobody said anything. The trio grabbed a table behind Rex and Lou.

Garrett raised the cap on his head and lifted one freckled cheek at Rex.

The dim lights from the bar caught his wide irises.

Rex ignored him. He and Lou drank for another solid hour. By this point, they were into shots of Beam with large beers to follow—Rex felt his legs get rubbery and go numb. Gladis faded in his mind. Instead, Garrett's face hovered before him, his voice bouncing inside Rex's head.

At the table behind Rex and Lou, Garrett told Lorrie dirty jokes. She kept asking him to quiet down, but Johnny laughed at all the stupid punch lines. He had a big, screechy laugh that made the bassist for Sugar Tits roll his eyes. Rex saw it all in the mirror behind the bar— Garrett delivering punch lines, Lorrie lifting a finger to her lips, Johnny groaning out his high-pitched laugh, and the bassist rolling his eyes like cue balls. He understood how the bassist felt. Johnny's laugh started to get on his nerves. Each time a laugh erupted and filled the bar, Rex's shoulders shuddered and his tongue pressed against the top of his mouth. Rex didn't know how much longer he could take it, the fucking pot dealer and his new pal. One more of these jokes and Rex was going to erupt.

Lou got his second wind and ordered a couple more beers and Beam. Sugar Tits finished their set and the Rolling Stones started up on the jukebox. Ray, the bartender, punched in the numbers for "Exile on Main Street" and all Rex wanted to do was hear the damn record and stare at Gladis across the bar while she gabbed with her girlfriends. Garrett wouldn't shut up and Johnny got louder and louder. "I'm getting real sick of this," Rex said.

Lou sucked air through his teeth. "I know exactly how you feel." He took one long swallow from his bottle and both he and Rex turned to stare down Johnny and Garrett. Blood surged in Rex's head. It pressed from his chest, into his neck and up around his eyes. "You mind telling those jokes in the privacy of your own home, Garrett?" Rex said. "If you have one."

Garrett pointed his grimy eyes at Rex and smiled. "I'm impressing the lady, can't you see that?" He tilted a beer bottle to his lips and set it back on the table. "How do you know my name anyway?"

"Impress her somewhere else," Rex said. He ran his tongue across his teeth, tasted hot bourbon. "Everyone knows who the lowlifes are—that's you."

"Lowlife, huh?"

"As low as it gets. Wouldn't work to fill your own stomach."

"I work every day."

"Is that what you think selling pot is, work?" Rex sniffed hard through his nose, sucked up the muffled conversation in the bar, the stiff odor of beer breath and cigarettes, the nasal whine of Mick Jagger sounding through it all. The bar crowd turned their eyes toward him, swung glassy looks to Garrett. "You're a lowlife bum. No job. No home. Shit, you may as well not exist."

Garrett removed his baseball cap and pointed it at Rex. "You two are the golfers up there in the neighborhood, aren't you?" His eyes drifted toward Johnny, pulled him into the conflict.

"Who gives a shit?" Lou said. He downed a slug of Beam, slammed the glass onto the bar. "What are you gonna do about it?"

"Something mean," Johnny said, "if you keep hitting the fuckers at my house."

Johnny's eyes looked like truth to Rex, the way they pointed sharp and hard. They were eyes that made Rex second guess his own toughness, but now the whole world was looking at them and he couldn't get away. Rex said, "That was weeks ago. You ever let things die?"

Johnny pressed his lips together and shook his head. "Fuck no, never."

"Let's finish it then." Rex slid off his bar stool. He straightened his back, felt sweat tingle on his upper lip and across his temples.

Johnny let another high-pitched laugh echo from his throat.

"Take this shit outside!" It was Ray, the bartender. He grunted a warning, "You don't want me to contribute, I promise."

They didn't test him. Nobody ever did. Garrett, Johnny, and Lorrie stood and walked through Old Miner's, out the front door and into the parking lot.

Rex finished his beer in one long gulp, patted his flat stomach.

He and Lou followed.

Outside, in daylight tinged with coming dusk, a sheriff's deputy was parked on the corner, just across the highway from Old Miner's. He leaned on the hood of his black and white and smoked a cigarette. It was any other day to him.

Rex eyeballed the deputy and looked toward Garrett, who stood alongside his blue Sentra. "It looks like your lucky day," Rex said.

Garrett's lips stretched across his teeth, peeled back over semi-gray gums. He climbed into his little blue car and rolled down the window. The grin stretched wider across his face. His teeth flashed yellow and he looked like a ginger-colored cat behind the wheel. Lorrie climbed into the back seat. She slumped, pulled her chin to her chest, tried not to catch Rex's eyes through the windshield. Johnny pulled his hat lower along his eyes. He raised his face to the sky and spit an arcing gob of thick saliva in the deputy's general direction. "That's what I think about all this," he said. "You two fucks better hit those golf balls in the other direction." He jumped into the passenger seat and slammed the door. Garrett backed out and the Sentra bounced across the parking lot, took off down the highway in a cloud of dust. The dirty little car's muffler rattled like a jigsaw. White smoke billowed from it.

"Exhaust leak," Lou said. "And that smoke says coolant leak. Bad gaskets."

Johnny leaned out the passenger side window and shouted into the wind. "Fuck you, poor boys! You'll go to hell!" The Sentra veered across the centerline and back into its lane. A moment later, it disappeared over the horizon.

The deputy leaned against his car and smoked his cigarette, one foot crossed over the other. He stood there and watched with sleepy eyes, like a ghost from some distant universe.

Rex shook his head. "Not even gonna pull them over, is he?"

"Nope—the guy doesn't give a shit."

"Johnny is starting to really piss me off," Rex said. "I'm almost done with him." He and Lou walked back inside and took their places at the bar. "What's Johnny gonna do, shoot us? He could have if he wanted to, but he won't." Rex ordered another beer and swilled it down to half, watched the liquid inside with dead eyes.

"He would have," Lou said, "if he had the balls."

"Right." The Rolling Stones record played louder and a song called "Shake Your Hips" came over the speakers. Gladis walked over to Rex and they hit the dance floor. It was the same as before. She pressed her body against him and he rubbed her neck. She smelled like daisies and cosmopolitan drink mix from behind the bar. This girl liked him. He didn't know why, but she did. Rex leaned over and shoved his nose into her brown hair. "I like your dress. You smell good." In his mind, Rex flashed to Garrett's yellow teeth and flapping red hair. *Man, I want that sucker's money. And I want him to feel some pain.* He thought about the coming week at work. No doubt, Garrett would meet Ralph one day, and that meant Rex could follow the Sentra, see where Garrett went on his rounds.

There was, of course, the problem of being recognized.

But Rex figured he and Lou would scare the guy—make him fear for his life—and that would kill any repercussions, make Garrett see it wasn't worth it to come after them. Rex started to see it like taxes. Garrett needed to pay his taxes, and he was going to pay them to Rex and Lou.

"You look good in those jeans," Gladis said. She tilted her chin toward him and batted her long eyelashes.

Rex snapped back into the moment. "So do you, lady."

Gladis giggled. Rex hummed the lyrics of the song deep in his throat. He put his lips to her earlobe and sucked on Gladis like she was a ripe, juicy peach.

"Where to now?" Garrett pursed his lips at Lorrie in the rearview mirror. He waited for her to respond, to smile or giggle. She could be so serious about shit. Things got heavy with her and that put Garrett in a bad mood. He wanted her out of it, back to being herself. What would he need to make that happen? "We gonna hit another dive bar, or what? Tell me you two aren't ready for bed."

Lorrie shook her head and turned from his reflection. "You two are such pricks. I thought we were going to have a good time. Next thing I know Ray is kicking us out of the place. I like Old Miner's—all the rest of the bars smell like water damage."

"You're not having a good time riding around with us?" Garrett turned his eyes back to the road, put his driver's side front tire on the edge of the dotted yellow line that split the highway.

"Not now, in the car. I wanted a few drinks."

"Plans changed, Lorrie. If that deputy wasn't there we would have been grinding those two punks into the parking lot. As it turned out, we had to get on our way." He met Lorrie's eyes in the mirror, blinked twice, and settled his gaze back on the road. "I can't have my car getting searched, not right this minute."

"Oh, right. Such tough guys, you and Johnny. I'd like to see you grind anybody into anything. Besides, you drive like shit. I'm surprised we didn't get pulled over, the way you speed all the time." Her voice turned sassy, a little playful. "You took a chance tonight and almost got caught."

"The deputy wasn't even in his car," Garrett said. "He was on a smoking break, probably planning to find himself a donut or two."

In the passenger seat, Johnny sighed and lifted the brim of his hat. He squinted at the small arc of Garrett's headlights as the Sentra swung through a series of long curves in the highway. A thousand cacti and misshapen boulders flashed and faded against dusk. "That kid, Rex. He needs an ass-kicking, a real pounding. I can't believe the balls on that kid, turning around like he wanted some of me—shit."

"He's asking for it," Garrett said. "I could kick him in the mouth. I swear to God."

"You two are horrible. Rex is alright. He's always been nice to me." Lorrie scanned the landscape beyond her window. "I remember he wrote me a love letter in high school. Said all this stuff about how he wanted to have kids and take them to the zoo."

Garrett and Johnny ignored her.

Johnny said, "You know what it is? It's the two of them together. They act like brothers. You get that tall one—Rex—you get him alone and he'll find out he's not so tough. Pisses me off, the way his eyes drape themselves all over the place."

"Like he's too good for everybody," Garrett said.

"Yes—that's exactly what it is. Like the guy never had a bad thought in his head."

"He's just like us. Only thing is, he denies it, tries to make himself feel honorable or whatever. I know his type. He's soft, man. Real soft."

"Hitting golf balls at my place, what the fuck is that anyway? Who golfs out here?"

"Shit," Garrett said, "it suits them two if you think about it. All high and mighty, out in their yard playing a gentlemen's game." He said the last two words with a high-pitched squeal.

"Rex was my first kiss," Lorrie said without meeting Garrett's eyes.

Silence filled the Sentra. It lingered for a mile of flat highway.

"You're kidding me. You got to be." Garrett leaned against his door, steered with one hand while, with the other, he massaged his chin. "That wimpy fucker?"

"He's not wimpy. Like I said, he's kind of a hard-ass."

"Alright. If you say so." Garrett paused before rattling off a few questions like gunfire. "How old were you? Was it him or you that started it? You like that fucker?"

"Oh, God. I was in the ninth grade and Rex was a senior. I thought his letter was sweet. It was just a little peck and it never happened again. It was nice though. I had a crush on him for a while after that."

"Really?" Johnny asked.

"Yes, really."

Johnny shook his head and, again, they rode in silence.

Garrett scraped his teeth together and tried not to feel the anger working itself into his head. After a few minutes, he caught Lorrie's eyes in the rearview mirror. She flashed her teeth at him and raised her eyebrows.

What the hell? It was only one kiss, right?

Everybody had to have a first one and there was no reason to hold it against her. Even if the guy was a prick. Besides, Lorrie was back to being herself, not all pissed off at the world. Garrett winked at her and smirked. "Where to, pretty lady? You said you wanted a good time, right?"

"Let's go to the dry lake bed and light a bonfire," Lorrie said. "It's beautiful out there. We can look at all the stars. First, though, we need a bottle of booze. I want to get drunk." She paused before adding, "and no fighting when we're out there either."

Johnny lowered his hat and grunted. "Dave's Liquor is up here on the left. You can stop in there for some booze. I'm thinking a little bourbon sounds like the right move. Goes well with a big fire, don't you two think?"

Sandoval, the night clerk, looked up from his book of crossword puzzles when they walked into Dave's Liquor, but he knew Johnny and paid little attention to the group. He brought the book back to his face, lifted his pen and jotted an answer.

"Hey, Sandoval," Johnny said. *I'm kind of a regular*

here, I guess. He tried not to make drinking a major habit, but it was habits that kept a man going. That's what he'd been telling himself for the last few years.

The clerk grunted at him.

He and Garrett headed toward the far length of the front counter, along the back of the store, and squinted at the bottom shelf bourbon bottles. Lorrie stood behind them with her arms crossed, tapped one foot against the tile floor.

"I like Evan Williams," Garrett said, "that alright with you two?"

"Let's get the big one, just in case." Johnny figured he could take the rest home if they didn't finish it. Besides, he was going to pay for it, treat everybody to a little something. He supposed he should try to make things up to Lorrie. He knew she was excited about hanging with him—her big brother—down at Old Miner's. They never spent time together. Mostly, they yelled at each other through her bedroom door. Ever since Daddy went north…

Lorrie moved toward the glass-doored cooler at the rear of the store, said over her shoulder, "I'm getting some Coke, too. And ice."

"We need cups, Sandoval. And that big bottle of Evan Williams," Johnny said.

The clerk slapped his book on the counter, stood, and ambled toward them. He lifted the bottle and brought it back to the register. Johnny and Garrett followed.

"I got some cups." Lorrie lifted a small bag of red go-cups and walked toward them with a liter bottle of Coke under her arm. She set the items on the counter. "A small bag of ice, too." She peered up at Garrett. "Bourbon and Coke."

"That's a girl's drink. I take it neat," he said.

"Aren't you tough."

Johnny pulled out his wallet and slapped down a twenty. "You two can flirt in private. Don't forget me—last thing I want is to play third wheel on a date night."

"We should have found you a lady for the night," Garrett said.

Johnny shook his head. He hadn't been on a date in a long while, but there was some knot inside him that wouldn't unravel—he didn't want anything to do with a woman right this second, but he wasn't sure why. Like many other things inside himself, he didn't understand that knot. He tried to ignore it. "I'm fine, just don't want to have to pry you two apart with a crowbar is all."

Sandoval punched open the register, scooped Johnny's change up, but his eyes swung over Johnny's shoulder as a man stumbled into the liquor store. They turned their heads. Johnny clicked his tongue as he looked at the man. He was a bum, wore a Mexican serape and a trucker's hat tilted like a triangle on his head. His face was clouded with bushy, black beard and his eyelids hung low across his irises. The man's pants were faded blue Levis with rips along his knees and thighs.

Sandoval shouted, "Fuck you! Out, get out. Not allowed here no more. Never again!" He slammed Johnny's change on the counter and pointed his whole hand at the man. "Fucking out!"

"What for?" The bum's voice came out jagged, tore across whiskey-soaked vocal chords. "I ain't do a damn thing to you."

"Stole my mouthwash. I saw the empty bottle," Sandoval said. "I saw it!"

The bum stood with his back hunched and jaw open;

the bottom of his mouth was missing a few important teeth. Lots of hard living in the man, Johnny could see that.

He said, "Well, damn you. I'll just take my business somewhere else then." He slammed his mouth shut and turned, stumbled back outside and out of view.

Sandoval shouted again as the man left, "Your son's looking for you!" He softened his tone. "Never buys nothing. No good for the business."

Johnny lifted his change from the counter. "What's all this about mouthwash?"

Sandoval swung his head back and forth. His chubby cheeks jiggled. "He stole it for drinking. Alcohol. You know?"

"No shit? The old man wants a buzz, huh?" This struck Johnny as funny, that the old man drank mouthwash to get his buzz, but it also hit him how sad and pitiful the thing was. Like, you have to drink mouthwash just to get drunk? My, oh my. "Get me one of them small bottles of Evan Williams, them little ones."

Sandoval brought it back and Johnny peeled a five-spot from his change and handed it across the counter. He got a few coins in return.

"Who is the guy?"

Sandoval blinked and looked outside through the windows. "Comes here all the time. Rex's father."

This perked Johnny. He tilted his head, lifted his hat brim. "Who?"

"Rex," Sandoval said. "You know, Rex. Tall guy with the Toyota?"

"Yeah—I know him. You saying that bum is Rex's daddy?"

Sandoval nodded. "Yes, but I want him out of here."

He lifted his book of crossword puzzles and coughed into the pages. "Sick of his stealing."

Lorrie said, "You going to support that bum's habit?"

Johnny turned and looked at her, held the small bottle of bourbon in the air. He waved it so tiny bubbles leaped to the surface. "Habit is all a man's got," Johnny said. "let's go and do ourselves a good deed."

Next to Lorrie, Garrett pushed his lips together, let them curl at the corners into small half-moons framing his teeth. He said, "Yep, a good deed indeed."

Xavier, alone for the night—at least, that's what he figured—twirled the pistol in the living room. The heavy gun flipped and spun along the first knuckle of his index finger. He was getting it. Yes, he was. Soon, Xavier was going to scare the shit out of Johnny. See how big brother liked that.

He stopped, let the pistol rest against his hip. Ear cocked to the air, Xavier listened for the sound of an engine. They'd come home in Garrett's car—he knew that. And Xavier also knew it wouldn't be good if Johnny caught him messing with Daddy's pistol. That would be time-out and extra chores and no cartoons.

He hated to be punished. He hated listening to Johnny.

But he loved his brother and sister. Xavier knew this was how it had to be, now that Daddy was gone, but he didn't like to feel small, to feel left out and lost.

Xavier walked to the window, peeled back the curtains and stared into the darkness. All he could see was his daddy's old fishing boat in the driveway, the one with the little outboard motor that always broke when they were on the water. Xavier remembered fishing with his daddy. They used to go summers, when the water up in the mountains started to warm, a month or so after the last snow melted. He remembered riding in Daddy's Chevy extended cab; a big, rattling truck that made Xavier feel like his teeth were going to fall out—it was like riding on a tractor. Daddy played Johnny Cash and snapped chewing gum. They stopped for soda, it felt like to Xavier, every few miles. His daddy, a tall man with yellow teeth, stomped into liquor stores with a grin on his face and snapped his fingers. "Point the boy here to the soda pop," he said. "Get him some sugar." Xavier always got grape soda. He sucked it down while they drove, that little fishing boat rattling behind them. In the truck's sideview mirror, he watched the life vests bouncing around inside and the fishing poles bobbing like twigs in the speed and wind.

The year before, Daddy took him up to the lake alone, taught him a new fishing knot and gave him a small pocket knife.

"You don't cut yourself with that, you hear?"

"I got it," Xavier said. He flipped the knife closed. It was tiny; a red, used Swiss Army knife with two dull blades, nail clippers and missing the toothpick. "What happened to the toothpick, Daddy?"

"I spit it at a horse that wouldn't move."

"Shit, daddy. We haven't seen a horse in weeks."

"What you mean? I rode a horse to work the other day."

"Hell, no. I know you didn't."

"You got a mouth on you, Xavier."

"I learned from the best." Xavier grinned at his daddy, showed his modest collection of tiny silver fillings. "Sorry about that."

"You better be. Look, Xavier—I need to tell you something about the next little while." His daddy reeled in a line, cast it out into the lake. The hook dropped like a pin and sent miniature ripples toward a few boats in the distance. "I ain't gonna be here for a while and I need you to listen to what Johnny says."

"Where you headed?"

"I got to go somewhere for a job. I'm hoping it's for only a little while, Xavier. I really am, but it might not be. I might be gone for quite a long time."

"Where you headed though?" Xavier might be punchy and wild, but he was smart. "You can't call us or nothing?" That was when Xavier knew it was for real, his daddy was going to be gone a long time. It was how the man's answer hit Xavier's ears; not the words themselves, but the way the words sounded.

"I could call, Xavier. I don't think I will though. Son, it might be that we don't talk for a long while. Now I want you to promise me that you'll listen to Johnny."

Xavier promised.

The next day, his daddy left and never returned. And that old fishing boat just sat there. It sat there all through the summer, into the winter, and it was still there. Xavier studied it, the way it sat there in the darkness like a weird-looking monster. That's what he should ask Johnny to do, take him and Lorrie on a trip to the lake. They could catch bass and catfish, fry it up in tinfoil with beer cans like Daddy did. Yeah, Xavier missed his daddy. He missed fishing, too. He let the curtains fall back over the window and walked to the center of the room. That's right, he needed to practice. Man, he wanted to scare Johnny. Xavier lifted the pistol, twisted his hand, spun the gun like it was a toy.

* * *

Rex and Lou were back home after a long day at Old Miner's. The alcohol had worn off for Rex and he perked up when he heard the sound of a small engine pull into Johnny's driveway. He walked to the window, peered through the curtains, and clicked his tongue against the roof of his mouth. "I think we do it tonight," he said. "I think we do it right fucking now."

"And they won't know who it is? The hell are you thinking, Rex?" Lou poured milk into a bowl of cereal and sank into the couch. "I thought we were doing this so they don't know it's us—so Garrett can't figure things out."

"No, we need to scare this motherfucker, put the fear of death into him. That's all he's gonna respond to, all he'll figure means anything." Rex pulled a beer from the refrigerator, popped the top and slammed the bottle cap against the floor. "I'm sick of knowing he doesn't do a damn thing. I'm sick of him showing up over there like he owns the damn world. And I'll tell you something else: I didn't like the way he looked at me this afternoon. And that's enough for me."

"What's got into you? You're talking about rolling this guy, about ripping him off. He's not just going to take it."

Rex leaned against the wall and his tall frame folded against itself like a skin-colored shadow. He slammed back the beer and grunted. A knot formed between his eyes, pressed itself against the inside of his head. He pinched the bridge of his nose with two fingers and grimaced. "I don't care. I have to hurt the fucker, I will." He lowered his hand and plunged his eyes into Lou.

"You in this with me, or what? I need you to help me— one guy can't do it. I'm going over there tonight and I'm going to pound that guy. I'm going to take whatever money he has on him. He's gonna get hurt, but that's just how it has to be."

Lou blinked a few times before he responded. "I'll roll with you, Rex. But I want to make sure you know how I feel. I don't want anybody hurt, not really. Look man, I know work sucks, that you can't—"

"—Stop there. It's not about that. It's about this guy." Rex lifted a finger and jabbed it in the direction of Johnny's house. "This guy, a guy who runs around with Lorrie like a pimp and who talks as if the whole world belongs to him. It's about that happening right over there, just down the road. Doesn't a thing like that bother you?"

"I try not to think about things like that."

Rex folded his mouth shut. Try not to think about it. Maybe that's the answer for all the crazy in this world. That's all we have in our power, to not think about it. Or, shit, we got the reverse. "I want to think about it. I love to think about it. Makes my heart beat fast and my brain race. Makes me want to act, to do—you know what I'm saying?"

Lou lifted a spoonful of cereal to his mouth. He slurped from it and chewed. "Part of me does, but there's another part of me that doesn't."

"What you up to, Rex?" Gladis purred over the phone to tease him. "You want to come by later? I'm still up, you know?"

"I might come by later. I had fun today. I miss you

already." Rex held a cold beer bottle to his forehead. He stood in the kitchen, talking on the wireless house phone. "We should go to dinner this week."

"I could make time. Have to arrange my late appointments at the salon, though. So let me know what night you want to do."

"Tuesday might be fun—break up the week a little bit."

"I hear that," Gladis said.

"Listen, you ever get sick of working every day? I mean, you get sick of pulling your weight all the time? I'm not saying work is bad. I get it. It's just, it seems so damn long and—fuck me—foreboding."

"I like what I do, Rex. It isn't work to me. But I get what you're saying."

"I'll give you a call a little later. Need to handle something around the house. I'll come by after that."

"Bring some wine. I can't wait to see you."

"Me too, and I will. I promise."

Rex hung up and dialed his mother.

"Hello?"

"Mom? It's me?"

"Hey, Rex. What are you doing this weekend, working?"

"Well, I'm off today. I have to go in tomorrow, but not until ten."

"You know, I never minded working on the weekends—it's slower."

"Not at a hardware store or lumber yard." Rex sipped from his beer and placed the bottle on the counter. He felt sick to his stomach—too much alcohol for one long day.

"Time goes by faster that way, am I right?"

"You are. Listen, Mom—"

"Is everything okay?"

"That's what I'm trying to tell you, Mom. It's just, I ran into Dad."

"Your father?"

"At Dave's Liquor Store. One morning before work. I meant to tell you when it happened, but I got busy and couldn't call. Well, I just didn't call. You know how it is."

"How'd he look?"

Rex waited a long time before speaking. When he could no longer stand his own silence, he said, "Well, Mom, I have to tell you, he didn't look too good."

The first smack on the roof woke Johnny from a light sleep. His eyes popped open and he shot glances around the living room. On the couch, the bum they picked up at Dave's Liquor Store was snoring in a deep sleep. "The fuck was that?" He leaned forward on his recliner and cocked an ear. Outside, nothing but desert silence. Down the hallway, soft guitar chords floated from Lorrie's room. *That's her damn make-out music.* Johnny stood and crossed the living room to open the front door. *I bet it's those bastards next door—more fucking golf balls.* As he thought it and squinted into the darkness, another smack came and a white golf ball bounced along the red ceiling tiles before landing in the dirt near Garrett's car. "Motherfuckers."

Johnny walked into the kitchen and came back a moment later with a .22 caliber rifle held across his chest. He marched outside into the thick darkness pierced by scattershot moonlight and lifted the rifle to his shoulder. He aimed as best he could and squeezed the trigger. In the distance, beyond his vision, a window shattered. He cupped a hand behind one ear and waited. No sound for a minute or so. What the hell. These bastards deserve it. Johnny levered the action and fired again. He hit metal—the bullet sparked on contact and zinged into the night. "Fuck you, Lou! Fuck the both of you!"

Another golf ball smacked the roof, bounced twice, and landed somewhere on the other side of Johnny's house. A shout came, "Go to hell, Johnny!"

"You son-of-a-bitch." Johnny lifted the rifle, but before he could squeeze off another shot, he felt the cold steel tip of a knife on the nape of his neck.

"Drop the rabbit gun, Johnny."

"Rex? You're taking this a bit far, aren't you?"

"Only as far as it needs to go. Drop it."

Johnny let the rifle fall into the dirt and grunted. "What are you gonna do, slice me up over a broken window?" Johnny stood still. He didn't want a knife plunged into the soft skin of his neck.

"Stay where you are now." Rex knelt and lifted the rifle. He pocketed the knife and nudged Johnny in the small of his back with the long barrel. "Let's get inside." The two men—barely men, little more than boys—walked toward the rectangle of light spilling from Johnny's house.

Rex smiled at Lorrie and Garrett as they came down the hall and into the living room. He held the rifle about waist high, the barrel pointed at them, but poised to swing back on Johnny who sat on the couch. Next to him, draped in the Mexican serape, was Rex's father. "Welcome to the party, lovebirds. This is a whole family thing. Come right in and take a seat next to trigger-happy Johnny here." Rex caught Lorrie rolling her eyes at him. Garrett stared him down, his eyes hard little rocks in their dark sockets. "Grab a seat real fast. We're gonna make this painless and easy." Garrett and Lorrie sat on either side of Johnny. Rex sauntered into the center of the living room and pressed the barrel of the rifle to Garrett's forehead. "We gonna make it easy?"

"Jesus," Garrett said.

"What the fuck are you doing, Rex?" Lorrie started to stand.

"Sit. Back. Down." Rex turned his head slightly, pointed his eyes at Lorrie. "Don't be stupid or make this difficult. It's happening and there's nothing your smart little boyfriend can do about it. You neither." He looked at Johnny. And then, with a plain expression, he looked at his own father who sat with his eyes pointed straight ahead, unmoving.

Garrett shook his head, the rifle barrel lifting slightly as he did so. "Lorrie, it's fine. You listen to this fuck-head...for now."

"What do you want, man?" Johnny's jaw clenched and sprouted hard knots along the ridges of his cheeks. "I'll give it to you—just tell me."

"I want a life I can stand. A little break every now and then. I want some money in my gawdamn bank account."

"Shit—I hear you, but I can't give you that. I'm just—"

"—not from you, Johnny," Rex said. He lifted his chin at Garrett. "From this son-of-a-bitch." He pressed the rifle harder against Garrett's forehead. "From this lazy, no good, pot-dealing son-of-a-bitch."

"Harsh, bro," Garrett said.

"You're such an asshole, Rex. What the fuck do you know about it?"

Rex's eyes glazed over and he glared at Lorrie. He swung the rifle toward her and pressed the barrel against her forehead. "I told you to shut the fuck up, Lorrie."

"Rex, come on, now—I'm sorry about shooting at you guys. I was just fucking around. You know that, man."

"Shut the fuck up!" In Rex's head, he felt anger knot and shoot down his synapses like the tiny vibrations of a piano string stretched too tight. His finger wrapped around the rifle's trigger. His lips stretched to reveal teeth going yellow and gums receding into the dark cave of his mouth.

Lorrie's eyes bulged. Her chin trembled and her pulse flashed through the veins of her neck. "Don't Rex. I'm sorry. I'm fucking sorry."

"I bet." He tightened his finger around the trigger. A twitch erupted above his right eye. Sweat ran down the sides of his face and dripped from his chin. "What the hell is he doing here?" He motioned toward his father.

Johnny blinked. "We picked him up at Dave's Liquor."

"He tell you who he was?"

Silence. The front door opened and Lou entered. He held the golf club in his hands. "You get it yet?"

"I was about to."

Garrett said, "I will kill both of you when this is over."

141

This gained Rex's attention. He set the rifle on Garrett, steadied it. "There's one man here who gets to do the killing, and it isn't you. Did he tell you who he was?" Rex squinted at Garrett. "You better say the truth."

"They were just giving an old man a drink," the man in the Mexican serape said. "We went out to the dry lake bed for a while, and then we came back here. I needed a place to sleep. That's all. They didn't know anything about me."

Lou leaned toward Rex and caught his eyes. "Get this guy's money and let's get out of here, man. You know this is bad. It's real bad, Rex."

"I want to know what they were doing with my father."

"We give to charity," Lorrie said. "Lots of people need help."

As Rex swung his gaze to Lorrie, he noticed his father's eyes go wide. Johnny, too, shifted beside the man.

And then pain exploded along the ridges of Rex's back, spread like a bruise down into his buttocks. He registered a loud noise, some distant crash, before his ears rang like church bells. His legs folded beneath him. His muscles—in every part of his body—turned to some viscous rubber. He collapsed onto the thin carpet and rolled his head to one side. From the floor, with a small shadow moving ahead of him, he whispered the question to his father.

"Where the hell have you been?"

The pain washed over him, a warm, blanketing wave.

From the dark shadows of the hallway, Rex saw a small boy move into the living room. He spun a pistol along the middle knuckle of his index finger, stopped it with his thumb. A smile crossed his lips. He shoved the pistol, hot barrel and all, into the waistband of his too-large skater shorts.

Like a bantamweight boxer, the boy raised both fists.

Then, slow and deliberate, he lifted the middle fingers on both his hands.

The warmth spread outward from Rex's back, through his torso, and toward his heart. He grunted and squinted at the small boy. The thought echoed in Rex's brain: *Dad, where the hell have you been?*

Rex felt hands on his shoulders, his neck, the top of his head.

Hands.

Those are hands. Whose hands?

And he knew. Rex smiled as his father's hands probed at his wound, rested firm against his slim belly, pressed into his shoulders.

He heard his father's voice.

"Keep breathing, son. Keep breathing. I've got you, son. I don't want you to worry. I'm going to do whatever I can. Please, son…keep breathing."

Bar Burning

"I don't care the guy has lived here fifty years—he ain't setting foot in my bar, not so long as I can make a fist and load a shotgun." The man who spoke these words had a red handkerchief tied around his neck—like some damn outlaw cowboy—and a thin mustache running across his upper lip. "Redbone ain't allowed in here. His kind ain't allowed in here."

From where he sat at the end of the bar, Packard watched the man's partner, a squat school-teacher type in plaid shirt and a dull green tie, nod his head and smile.

Packard lifted a glass of bourbon to his lips and drained it.

He didn't know who Redbone was, and he didn't need to know.

His kind ain't allowed in here. That phrase bounced around in Packard's head. The two men nodded at each other and smiled. It was a weeknight; the bar was empty aside from these two talky beer guts and Packard.

The squat teacher said, "It's not a matter of political correct, pure and simple. No sir, it's about what's right. Am I right?"

"You are, fuck yes," the other man said.

The squat teacher again, "You got a right to refuse service. Race, creed, color, religion. None of that matters in the face of your rights. Business is gawdamn business. Nothing anybody can do about it."

The other man tugged at his red handkerchief, untied it. He folded it into a small square and dabbed at beads of sweat on his forehead. "What I say, goes. It's my place. That's all there is to it. And it don't have to do with the color of the man's skin. Oh, hell. Maybe it does—maybe that's part of the reason, but it's not the only damn reason." He ran the handkerchief over his mustache and coughed without covering his mouth.

More rapid nods and stupid smiles.

Packard swung around and studied the bar. A few wobbly wooden tables and a line of booths with ripped vinyl seats along the back wall. The digital jukebox glowed like a lantern. In the deepest corner, a Street Fighter arcade game spat flashing lights and fighting words. Sonic boom. Sonic boom. Sonic boom. The bar's walls were damp plywood papered with handwritten flyers for dog fights and house parties. He sniffed and caught the odor of matted fur and liquor cut with dirty water. Packard concluded: This place is a shit hole.

He swung his gaze back to the talky beer guts and smirked.

"Can we help you?" It was the squat teacher talking. His double-chin flapped beneath his little round mouth. "Are we bothering you?"

"Yeah," said the other guy, "you got some kind of problem?"

Packard lifted his empty glass and held it at arm's length. "Tell me how much this place is worth." The bar's dim light glinted off the glass.

"Who the fuck are you?" The man ran the red hand-kerchief across his mustache again. "Who the fuck are you?"

Packard slammed his glass onto the beer-stained floor. Shards of glass rained beneath the wobbly tables. When Packard looked up, a red handkerchief was laying on the bar and a double-barreled shotgun was aimed at his head. *Oh, I see, Mr. Shotgun.* "I'm your last customer." Packard stood and walked toward the door, clenched his hands into hard fists. He imagined the two men squinting at the reaper on his motorcycle vest, its ghostly face flashing between a grin and a smirk.

"You don't come back now," the man with the mustache said. He thumbed back the shotgun's hammers for dramatic effect. The dull clicks echoed. "I'll shoot you in your belly if I have to."

Packard stopped. The phrase drifted into his head again: *His kind ain't allowed in here. It don't have to do with the color of the man's skin. Oh, hell. Maybe it does.* Packard shook his head slowly, pushed the creaky door and walked into the warm desert air.

It's a need—destruction.

A man has to make things burn. He's got no choice about that. But what he burns, that's what tells you who he is. Packard turned in circles and took in the shadowed desert. He tried to memorize the jagged mountain outline framing the sphere of sandy horizon. The range was all serrated edges and saw-toothed gaps sketched in silver moonlight. He kept turning—his scuffed black boots made half-moons in the dirt—until his eyes settled on the ramshackle structure that housed the shit hole bar.

A thing worth hating is a thing worth burning.

He crossed the empty two-lane highway toward his motorcycle.

It was a flat-black Harley Davidson with chrome pipes. Packard flipped open one of his leather saddlebags and yanked a bottle half-full with bourbon from the bag's bottom. He held the bottle to the moon-light and closed one eye. He twisted off the cap and took a long swig. The burn felt good. He set the bottle in the dirt. Packard dug deeper into the saddlebag. He moved aside a Colt .45 handgun—it was wrapped in an army-green T-shirt—and came out with a thin paper-back book. The book's cover said: *The Art of Worldly Wisdom.* The pages were marked with black ink in Packard's unreadable shorthand. He'd circled certain words and underlined others. At times, he'd drawn light-ning bolts and bullets in the white, open spaces between chapters.

Packard tore the cover and the first few pages from the book. He threw the rest of it back into the saddle-bag. *A thing worth hating is a thing worth burning.* He rolled the cover and the rest of the pages into a tight spiral and slid a few of the pages from the spiral until they made a thick candle-like wick. The wick went into the bourbon bottle. Packard pulled a silver lighter from his pocket.

Back across the highway.

He stood in the little half-moons his boots made a few minutes before. He flicked the lighter and touched the flame to the once-cover of *The Art of Worldly Wis-dom.* The pages caught and orange-yellow fingers licked at the air and spit heat into Packard's face. He slipped the lighter into the front pocket of his Levis and ran his fingers through the white hairs of his beard. He screwed his lips into a smooth S.

Packard lifted the flaming bottle, reared back, and threw it.

An orange-yellow streak arced through the silvery desert light.

In the distance, the jagged mountain range stood its ground.

Packard rolled back on the Harley's throttle as the red handkerchief man stumbled outside into the dirt. *He can't even hold his cut-rate liquor.* The man looked up at the crown of flames in the sky, a twisting watermark of fire still growing.

Packard pressed his lips together and squinted at the man. He steered his hog onto the highway. From the corner of one eye, Packard saw the man turn toward him and raise both his hands. He gave Packard the one-finger salute. "Fuck you," the man screamed, "I'm coming for you and I'm gonna kill you, hippie!"

Packard shifted into second gear.

The hog's rear tire chirped. Packard and the bike faded into darkness, swallowed by the empty ribbon that was the highway.

After three miles, Packard turned east onto a dirt road. He steered the Harley through a couple of rough patches—he placed his boots on the sand and rocks to balance the bike—and entered a single-track trail. The trail ran straight for close to a mile between two rocky peaks. It was a gradual ascent and he'd ridden it many times. Packard feathered the throttle and took things slow. The Harley wasn't made for dirt, but he sure as hell wasn't going to leave it out where some desert punks could lift it into the back of a truck.

These were his wheels, man. This was his thunder.

He reached camp and switched off the bike. Packard swung a flashlight beam across the sand and checked for footprints. He found only one set—his own size twelve boots. The camp was a flat, sandy outcropping overlooking a narrow canyon. The canyon's smooth granite surfaces opened into the desert below like a wide mouth. Up here, Packard was east of The Mesa—the lone stretch of high desert he'd made his home—and he could see the highway running crossways to the horizon until it fell off toward town. From his chair beside the fire, Packard watched people who lived on The Mesa drive up from town like tiny ants—they flowed from the place where the highway disappeared over the desert's sharp edge.

And from his chair beside the fire, Packard watched the bar burn to the ground.

The flames were visible, though by now they'd shrunk to a dim glow. Sirens revolved and flashed down there; he'd at least given the volunteer fire department something to go home and tell their wives about. That red handkerchief bastard and his squat teacher friend deserved what they got. Packard watched the flames until they subsided. When they were gone, when the sirens had stopped flashing and the desert's only sound was the echo of a coyote's howl, Packard crawled into his army-green tent and closed his eyes.

* * *

A beam of sharp sunlight and heat filtered through the tent's flapping ripstop onto Packard's bearded face. He opened his eyes and turned away from the light, but the tent was too hot. No more sleep for him. He sat up, pulled on his vest, fastened his Levis, and coughed into his fist. He thought of the bar burning; in his mind, he saw the flames dancing and turning and twisting against the star-bright darkness above the desert. It was no loss—the bar. No, it was a favor he'd done for the world. These days, he was in the business of doing the world favors. Even though that sometimes meant the world didn't know what favors it needed. *You're no saint, you son-of-a-bitch. Don't make yourself into a thing you're not. All you did was start a fire.* But sometimes starting a fire is all it takes. Packard knew that. More than that, he believed it. Maybe he was misguided or foolish. Maybe he was evil in his own special way, but he carried with him some sense of justice—or properly dispensed injustice. Inside him, there was always a reverse magnetism charged by opposite poles—right and wrong.

You do what feels right, and usually that's fine.

Packard crawled outside the tent and stood in midday sun. His bare feet made imprints in the sand. He lifted his arms toward the sky and stretched. Below him, the camp dropped into a canyon of granite and shadows. Down where the desert lay unraveled and reflective beneath the sunlight, Packard spotted three ravens circling. Patient and persistent, they traced flat spheres in the sky over their target. He raised a hand over his eyes and watched. Soon, the ravens touched down behind a stand of yucca trees. Packard lost sight of them.

Something dead behind those trees. Something lost out there.

Packard pulled his boots from inside the tent. He turned them upside down and shook. Small pebbles and dirt fell at his feet. No spiders. No snakes. No dead things.

Time to put these boots on and start another day in the desert.

"You hear about Sketchy's bar?"

"Burned to ash. I drove by. He don't own that land neither. Looks like Sketchy needs a new profession."

"Place was a shit hole anyhow."

"Didn't even have a pool table."

"Right. What kind of bar doesn't have a pool table?"

"The kind gets burned down, I guess."

"I heard it was that hippie did it—the one that rides the Harley."

"Yep. Not sure I'd describe him as hippie, though. More like a demon or a drifter or, hell, I don't know. Something like that. Sketchy was down here on Thursday. How I heard about his place. He comes in here all red-faced and sweaty. You know how he gets. Asks me if I sell grenades—you believe that?"

"Grenades?"

"Yep. Like the Marines carry. Jesus. I asked him was he looking for a job with the feds. Maybe he's trying to set me up, you know? Do I sell grenades. Jesus. He got all pouty like he does, kept wiping his mustache. Tells me he's willing to pay whatever it takes to get a grenade. One will do, he says."

"And?"

"I told him to fuck off."

"You think he's going after the hippie?"

"No doubt about it. Funny, he buys more shells for his double-barrel. But he also gets himself a nice .22, a Winchester I had here on pawn from Marl."

"The greasy bastard lives in that house his grandma left him?"

"That's him. Dropped that Winchester here a few months back. I think he forgot about it. Anyhow, Sketchy bought himself the Winchester and a shit ton of shotgun shells. Like he's going into the bush or something. Jesus."

"Maybe we'll have a dead hippie on our hands soon."

"That, or a dead Sketchy."

Sketchy looked down the barrel of his new Winchester .22 rifle and closed one eye. He centered the watermelon between the sights and rested his finger on the trigger. "I'll shoot this fucker through and through." The low evening sun flashed against Sketchy's mud-brown eye. The watermelon was fifty yards out and resting atop the stump of a dead and fallen Joshua tree. Sketchy was practicing. "It ain't...gonna...be...a problem."

"You got this one," squat teacher said. He was a teacher—he taught tenth-grade civics at the high school in town. He wore a different shade of plaid this day, but his tie was the same dull green. His students called him Mr. Masters. "You got the eye for the prize."

Sketchy opened both eyes and looked at his pal. "Masters, would you shut up?" He bent his head to the rifle and settled his finger on the trigger, squeezed. The report echoed across the desert, but the watermelon sat there all green and shiny and round. Sketchy missed. "Fucking hell."

"I think you need to hold your breath when you fire," Masters said. "I saw it in one of those movies with that actor—the guy who has the scar on his lip. The one with the mean eyes."

"You talking about Tom Berenger?"

"That's him. He's in a few of those kinds of movies. Plays a special forces guy and shoots the shit out of everybody. I think he holds his breath."

"*Sniper* is what they're called, the movies. One, two, and three." Sketchy lifted his head and studied the watermelon. He propped the rifle on his knee and licked his index finger. He lifted the finger and tested the wind. He didn't feel a thing. "Okay, Masters. I'll try to hold my breath." He raised the rifle and bent his head to the stock.

Packard rolled back on the Harley's throttle and shot forward into the sunset. He spotted a white pickup truck rattling down the highway at him and drifted the Harley closer to the yellow centerline. Packard liked the feel of wind created by a vehicle passing in the opposite direction, a hard wall of force followed by pure, weightless nothing. He liked crossing from one thing to the next, the way it felt. *Maybe that's what death feels like.* The image of the three black ravens touching down earlier that day surfaced inside him. *Maybe you'll find yourself prey for the scavengers one night.* His lips stretched above his teeth. Packard touched the Harley's front tire to the solid yellow line and grinned at the pickup truck. It barreled at him, a rattling assemblage of white metal and rubber and glass. The truck's horn sounded, but Packard kept his tire humming along the yellow line. *Let's do this, sucker.*

The truck's driver pumped the horn and steered toward the road's edge, the spot where pavement dropped off into sandy shoulder. The two vehicles passed with only two feet or so between them. Wind shot between the gaps of Packard's teeth. His lips rolled and twisted. Stringy, dark brown hair dangled behind him, tentacles in the hot air.

Time stopped for a moment as the wind gave way to nothing. Packard felt the dead space of weightless speed, the lightness he imagined death might hold, the pure absence that should have filled him with dread, but didn't. And then the wind was back. Packard steered the Harley into his lane and shot forward into the sunset.

Sketchy's mustache bristled. "And now comes the fucking wind. Just what I need." He pressed his lips together and bent his head to the Winchester's sights. The watermelon was still there, perfect and round and green.

Masters said, "Maybe it's the opposite. Maybe you let out all your breath and hold it like that. Yeah—I think that's what the guy does in the movies."

"I'll do whatever it takes to shoot this fucker."

"We should eat the thing. It's innocent. Why the hell are we shooting it?" The tie around his neck fluttered in the wind, an appendage shooting from beneath his chin. Masters reached out and grabbed it with two fingers, threw it over his shoulder. "I could eat some watermelon."

"It mimics the size of a human head. That's why we're shooting it."

157

"That's a big human head."

"Shit!" Sketchy screamed. "I'm trying to concentrate on this bitch and you won't shut up. Do you like the sound of your own voice that much?" He lowered the rifle and glared at Masters. Sketchy's eyes seemed darker somehow and hard as razors. He held Masters in his gaze for close to a minute. Then he lifted the rifle back to his shoulder and bent his head against it. He closed one eye, sighted in and fired. The round plunged into the tree stump, a few feet below the watermelon. "Shit! Fuck! Bastard!" Sketchy slammed the Winchester into the dirt and let loose an animal scream. He turned, opened the door to his minivan, and pulled out the double-barreled shotgun. He opened the breech—it was loaded. He slammed it shut. Sketchy stomped toward the water-melon. Dust rose from his heels and drifted on the wind.

"The hell?" Masters held his hands out in front of his body as if to beg for money. "I don't think you'll get that close to the guy. I really don't."

Sketchy kept up his march toward the watermelon. About ten yards out he stopped, lifted the shotgun to his shoulder and fired. The report sounded like thunder and hard metal snapping at the same time. The watermelon exploded. Shards of green shell blasted into the air and blood-pink pulp fell in wet, goopy clumps. The shot's echo died on the wind. "Fuck, yes! Ahhhhh!" Sketchy lowered the shotgun and lifted his head to the sky. He closed his eyes, let the last drops of sunlight filter through his eyelids.

"Nice shot," Masters said. He lowered his hands, shoved them into the pockets of his khakis. "That thing makes for a good show."

Sketchy marched back to the minivan. Again, little

clouds of dust sifted from his heels. He threw the shotgun into the back seat. Masters bent and plucked the Winchester from the dirt. He blew the dust off the stock and barrel, handed it to Sketchy who threw it in with the shotgun. Both men turned to stare at the spot where the watermelon had been, the empty half-tree without its shiny green watermelon head. "I told you I'd get it. All it takes is practice."

Masters nodded and smiled. "You want to go get us some beers?"

"Carbs, carbs, and more carbs. That's all you ever buy."

Packard dropped a package of multi-grain bagels into his red handheld basket. Even outlaws and outcasts and exiles needed their groceries. He turned his head and looked at the woman who'd spoken to him. She was in her mid-forties—he could tell from the wrinkles at the corners of her eyes—and shorter than most, maybe a little over five feet tall. She had her hands on her hips. Her black polo shirt clinched her lithe torso and disappeared beneath the slim waistband of her bleached Levis. She had grass stains on her knees. Her black Doc Marten boots were scuffed and the soles caked with dried mud. A rectangular, orange name tag pinned to her shirt said Gypsy. Packard wondered, is that her real name? "You watch me every time I come in here?"

"Yeah, well—it's my job to make sure the customers eat healthy," she said.

"I thought it was your job to ring me up and bag my groceries."

"I go above and beyond. And you, mister, need the help." She walked over to Packard's basket and fingered each of his items. "Multi-grain. Okay, that's fine. Old Forester Bourbon." She paused for a moment, let her pink fingernails scratch at the bottle. "I'm okay with the bourbon, too. This six-pack of beer needs to go, though. No beer when you have bourbon—it's just empty carbs." She tilted her head at Packard.

He noticed one thin strand of brown hair across her nose. She pursed her lips and blew it to the side, used a pink fingernail to tuck it behind her ear. Her eyes came through as green to him, but in the store's light he couldn't be sure. "No beer, huh? That's rough on me."

"You need to get some apples," she said. "Grapes, too. And buy some damn vegetables. This looks like the menu at a bachelor pad. You're a grown man, aren't you? You know your food groups? Or you want me to draw you a chart? I'll draw you a chart. Maybe that'll help." She bit the corner of her bottom lip to hide the smile stretching across her smooth face.

"I am a grown man, yes."

"Then act like it."

"You got another job?"

"Just this one—I'm a career girl."

"Loyal," he said.

"As can be."

"What time you get off today?"

"You asking me out?"

"I'm telling you when I'm going to pick you up."

"Give me thirty minutes." She flipped Packard's vest aside and placed the flat palm of one hand against his stomach. "I'll meet you outside."

Packard nodded and brushed past her. "I'll be there," he said without looking back. The red handheld basket swung beside him.

"Don't drink that bottle of bourbon. Not before I get my lips on it."

"You ever been on a bike?"

Gypsy rolled her eyes at Packard and scanned the parking lot. "You want me to sit up front? Of course I've been on a bike—I can probably ride better than you."

Packard grinned and tapped the orange name tag with one fat index finger. "That your real name? Or just some cute handle for all the boys?"

Gypsy scanned the parking lot again and climbed onto the Harley behind Packard. She whispered into his ear, "Some names we just can't shake." She wrapped her arms around his waist and squeezed. "You better have some bourbon left for me."

Packard fired up the Harley and gassed the throttle.

Thunder, baby. Pure thunder.

Sketchy's minivan thumped along the dirt road. It creaked and moaned. In the passenger seat, Masters pressed one hand against the roof and used the other to grip the center console. "Jesus, Sketchy—you mind slowing down a bit?" He peered over his shoulder, through the minivan's tinted back window, and saw the cloud of dust they left behind them. He looked back at Sketchy.

The man was wound up too damn tight.

All pissed off about his bar burning.

Sketchy gripped the steering wheel with both hands and stomped on the gas pedal. His mouth was screwed up into itself; it looked like a piece of newsprint crumpled into a ball. His dark sunglasses reflected the desert's pitted landscape. "I swear to god I'm going to kill that man."

"Take it easy, Sketchy. Don't kill me in the process." The minivan hopped over a pile of small rocks. Masters bounced in his seat and his head slammed against the window. "God, pal. I thought we were headed to get us some beers."

Sketchy gave it more gas and power-slid through a long bend in the road. "Let's go get us some hippie blood. That's what we're gonna do—go get us some red-hot hippie blood. That son-of-a-bitch thinks he can burn my place down and get away with it, just keep riding his hog around like some kind of super-action-comic hero. Not up here, not on The Mesa." Sketchy powered the minivan through a stretch of soft sand and grinned beneath his mustache.

Masters gripped the center console, pressed his head back against the seat and closed his eyes.

"What the hell you looking at out there?"

"I just saw Gypsy get on the back of that drifter's bike. Right outside Food-4-Less. She hopped on like they're out for a date."

"No shit? Sketchy's Gypsy—his ex-wife?"

"You know any other girls called Gypsy?"

"No, I do not. I'll tell you what, that hippie, drifter, whatever you want to call him—he's got a hell of a fight coming his way. First, he burns down Sketchy's bar. Second, he takes Sketchy's old, old lady for a ride. What's third?"

"A dark hole for somebody. That's what's next."

* * *

Gypsy clinched her arms around Packard's midsection. She felt comfortable putting her hands on him, like somehow they were meant to be there. Packard pressed the bike into a long turn that put them on the two-lane highway. Gypsy closed her eyes. The wind pelted her eyelids and whipped her hair behind her head. Packard shifted into fourth gear and they settled into the dusk's slow burn, headed toward Gypsy's house at The Mesa's far northern end. She had a three-bedroom house all to herself with a cactus garden and an above-ground pool. Not bad, but it was hell getting to and from work each day. Maybe she should get herself a bike. A lighter model no doubt, but how badass would she look riding a Harley through town?

Real badass.

They crested a rise and Gypsy opened her eyes. Out of instinct or habit or hatred, she looked left and squinted into the approaching night. There it was, those charred cinders of Sketchy's old bar. She grinned and placed her lips against Packard's right ear. "Let's stop for a sec."

Packard slowed and pulled onto the road's shoulder, flipped the automatic shut-off switch. The engine died and the desert's odd silence filled their ears. "Not much to see here."

And there wasn't. Not anymore. Where the bar used to stand, the view of the desert was restored. The jagged mountains stood in the distance and the landscape was dotted with Joshua trees and semi-round boulders piled atop each other. The bar was pure ash and burned wood. A few tufts of singed paper drifted in the wind. The concrete foundation was still there, but everything else was gone. Gypsy swept her eyes over the destruct-tion. "You have no idea how happy I am to see those ashes."

Packard grunted. "Why's that?"

"Some things need to burn, that's why." She hesi-tated for a moment. "My ex owned the place. He's a cheat and a snake. I guess that's why, too."

Packard nodded, cleared his throat and said, "You ready?"

Gypsy placed her lips against the side of Packard's neck, left a wet spot. She whispered into his ear, "Let's roll."

Packard turned the key. He flipped a switch.

The Harley rumbled beneath them.

Sketchy slid the minivan onto the highway and floored it. "I'm going to find the son-of-a-bitch tonight, Mas-ters. I swear to you I'll find him and I'm going to put that shotgun to work."

Masters looked down at his hands. His knuckles were white from the ride along the dirt road. "Maybe you should think about this some more. I mean, this guy did seem like kind of a badass the other night."

"I should have shot him then."

"But you didn't. And now he knows you're looking for him. You think he won't carry some kind of gun? You think he won't be ready when you roll up on him?"

Sketchy said, "It needs to get done. That's all there is."

"Look, I'm telling you—"

"Shut your mouth."

"What?"

Sketchy said, "Shut your mouth and do it now."

Masters twisted in his seat. "Man, you're losing it. I didn't do shit to you. Tell me why, wait, what the fuck?"

Sketchy slammed on the brakes and the minivan slid to a stop. The tires screeched and the smell of burned rubber seeped into the vehicle. Sketchy lowered his dark sunglasses along the bridge of his nose. His eyes were like razors again, sharp and dangerous. "Get out of this car. Just get out."

"We're ten miles from town—what the hell?"

"Get out. Do it now."

"Sketchy—"

"You're walking home."

Masters sank into his seat. He peered at Sketchy with shiny eyes. "I've got to work tomorrow, man."

"Out."

Masters opened the door. He unlatched his seatbelt and stepped onto the pavement. He leaned back into the minivan and met Sketchy's dangerous eyes. "Man, you need some kind of help. That bar is gone and there's nothing you can do about it. You need to get that through your head."

Sketchy pressed the dark sunglasses back up his nose with one finger. He pushed his lips together. His thin mustache twitched. He slammed his foot against the gas pedal and the minivan shot down the highway. The bald tires shrieked. The passenger door slammed shut under the force of the minivan's momentum.

Masters lunged backwards to save his toes. "Fuck." He stood in the center of the highway and watched Sketchy's red taillights fade, like two animal eyes fading along the folds of a shadow.

* * *

Packard spotted the headlights first. The beams came up over a rise in the highway and swung toward them like a searchlight. He feathered the throttle and leaned backward into Gypsy. He said, "You want to have a little fun?" Her brown hair whipped into his face. He tasted split-ends in his mouth.

Gypsy put her lips to Packard's ear and said, "Only if it's dangerous."

Packard steered the bike toward the yellow centerline. Silver moonlight outlined the desert and the highway and the two riders on the motorcycle. They sped toward the headlights, two beams growing brighter every second.

Sketchy noticed the vehicle approaching him on the highway. One headlight. He still had his dark sunglasses on—night be damned—and squinted to make certain. *Couldn't be, there's no way that's him.* But Sketchy had a feeling, a vague notion that meeting out here, on the dark highway, was the only way a thing like this should happen. Somehow, it felt right. He wouldn't run the hippie down, though. No—not like that. Too easy to do it that way, too damn simple. Sketchy saw flames in his head. Heat blasted against his face, hard and heavy.

He was back there, in front of his bar burning. He watched the thick orange fingers of flame lick at the wood. He heard the soft crackle rising to a fevered scream, flames devouring wood. Those screams—the screams of a life dying—echoed inside him. He fell to his knees and plunged his fingers into hard dirt. In his head, again and again, Sketchy watched his bar burn to the ground. He forced himself to shake the memory. He blinked hard and focused on the lone headlight. Sketchy pressed harder on the gas pedal.

Packard put the Harley's front tire on the yellow center-line. They were hurtling toward the headlights now. He let his eyes drift to the speedometer. It inched upward in its arc. Around his waist, Packard felt Gypsy's arms tighten. Her fingers scratched at the skin on his stom-ach. She was in it with him. He knew she wouldn't let go or scream at him to stop. They had the same prob-lem, Gypsy and Packard. They were unmoored, fitful beings who only knew the road as home. They only felt alive when driven forward into motion, escape, uncer-tainty. A hundred yards from the headlights, Packard rolled back on the throttle and their silver outline sped forward, toward hard wind and the emptiness beyond.

Sketchy made out Packard's waving hair as the Harley entered his headlights' perimeter, but he made out another shape, too. Brown hair waving in the wind, a dainty figure hidden behind the big man's vested frame. A woman. And before Sketchy could veer to his right, the motorcycle was there, just left of his windshield. The hippie's rotten face filled his driver's side window. It came at him like a demon, a Halloween mask sketched from moonlight and flame and mortal skin. Sketchy sneered at the demon face and the ungodly roar boom-ing from the Harley. And then he saw her—the woman. He recognized the pert, smooth face and black-collared polo clinging to the slim body. Her fingernails, prying and gripping at the hippie's black vest, shone bright pink.

Sketchy knew. It was her.

The van's tires screeched before Packard saw it reflected in his sideview mirror. Then the vehicle came into view. The taillights flashed red and the awkward shape shifted and slid across the highway. Packard slowed and stopped. He turned to see the minivan spin a full revolution. It ended up pointed right at Packard and Gypsy.

The engine revved and the van hurtled toward them, covering half the distance in a few seconds then slid to a screeching halt.

A voice filtered through the van's screech, a brief scream above everything. Packard sensed motion from the minivan, heard the driver's door pop open and a series of frantic footsteps. He turned to see the cowboy from the bar running at them. His eyes were covered by dark sunglasses and the sweat on his forehead reflected moonlight. In his hands, he gripped the double-barreled shotgun.

"Don't fucking move, hippie!" The guy bent to one knee. He aimed the shotgun like he was holding a bazooka. He was about thirty yards out, dead center in the roadway.

"Oh, Jesus—get us out of here," Gypsy said. Her voice was breathy in Packard's ear, almost vacant the way it drifted out of her.

Packard dropped the bike from neutral into first. He let the clutch slip and burned the throttle with his opposite hand. Sand and gravel spun from beneath the

Harley's rear tire. Engine noise drowned out the cowboy's next shouts. The Harley shot forward like a flat-black bullet.

The man would fire the shotgun—Packard had no doubt about that, and he imagined the warm burn of pain spreading through his body.

Will it be like nothing, like the emptiness beyond the wall of wind?

Instead, he only felt hot desert air.

Packard glanced at the sideview mirror.

The shotgun was aimed at them. Sketchy's shoulders were pulled in tight against his chest. Behind him, the minivan's headlights cast the scene in silhouette, a relief in framed off-yellow. Two blasts sounded from the gun, thunder booming through silence. But Packard and Gypsy were gone, bent hard into the wind toward endless darkness.

Packard dropped the bike into second, third, and fourth gear. Behind them, the minivan's headlights faded into a small circle of light.

Masters pulled the loafer from his right foot. He turned the shoe upside down and sand cascaded to the pavement. "Dammit. This is bullshit." He slipped the loafer back on and did the same thing with the other. More sand. More damn sand.

He started shuffling toward town again. He already had fat white blisters on his feet—no way he could walk ten miles. He couldn't do much. Never had been able to do much. Masters knew he was a sidekick, a secondary character in life. He went to college, got mediocre grades, learned to play a few songs on a keyboard—

what his buddies called vagina rock—and bought himself a Honda Cruiser motorcycle he was too scared to ride.

I can't even lift the thing. How can I ride it down the highway?

You can grow a pair of balls, that's how.

But Masters never would grow a pair of balls. Not in the next life, and sure as hell not in this one. He plodded along and kept his eyes on the pavement. And when that harsh roar—the thunder crack sound of horsepower—came at him from across the desert, Masters panicked. *It's that hippie.* The highway was still dark. It curved eastward in a slow bend. Masters judged the Harley as a mile or so away from him. No way he wanted that guy to see him alone. He decided he should hide. He plunged into the desert with his loafers and khakis and ugly plaid shirt. A low-growth cactus jutted through his khakis and into his right shin. He bent, picked the spikes from his skin, and walked a few hundred feet.

The roar grew louder. A moment later, the lone headlight cracked the darkness and Masters raised a hand to shield his eyes. He found himself thinking of that night—the bar burning. He heard the same sharp roar of the Harley engine, but when he stumbled outside behind Sketchy, the engine noise didn't scare him. The fiery orange flames did. He imagined burning up like a piece of newspaper, a man turned to black ash and pointless words. It was then that he knew what he was, so pointless as to be invisible.

Well, almost.

The headlight pivoted to the highway. Masters lowered his hand and watched the Harley roar toward him. The hippie had a woman with him. Masters could see her brown hair whip against the creamy skin of her face. And then it came to him. It wasn't the fire or the threat of death that scared Masters. No, it wasn't those things at all. It was the hippie that scared him.

The hippie was the fire. The hippie was death.

That face, the young skin with its pure white beard. It unsettled Masters.

The Harley passed and the roar faded. Masters watched the taillight disappear beyond a rise. When it was gone, he looked down at his crotch where a large wet stain grew and grew and grew. *If I only I could grow a pair of balls.*

You turn into something you never intended.

An ex-wife. A failed mother. A Food-4-Less stock girl. You turn into that old cliché that haunts the women in your family. At forty-four years old, you rub your hands together and practice yoga and smoke pot and drink booze like water. You watch the wrinkles at the corners of your eyes spread until they run forever down your face. Ah, you are what you hoped to avoid— the small-town girl living a life that bleeds into a forgotten story. Gypsy knew that's what would happen. She'd be forgotten. All the mistakes she made in her years added up to more than the good she'd done. Her daughter, estranged and living some life in a city. Her ex-husband, crazy and fitful, a horrible man with a double-barreled shotgun.

Gypsy watched the desert landscape slide beside her. She had an odd sensation: the world seemed to spin while she remained still on the Harley. She knew they were moving forward, pressing faster and faster against folds of speed, but she felt motionless. And the brush and cacti and Joshua trees pointed at the sky, fingers accusing somebody up there. Night pressed at the horizon and Gypsy wished she could see farther, deeper into the desert. The ground slid, slippery and liquid, beneath the Harley. This is how the years feel—how life moves, unhinged and listless.

Gypsy leaned into Packard, tried to anchor herself to him.

The question of who he was bobbed in Gypsy's throat, scratched at the back of her mind. But what kind of right did she have to ask questions? All the right in the world, sister. Oh, but then he'll want to know everything about you. He'll want to know it all. One question would lead to the next and the next and the next.

And the only real answer would be more questions.

Gypsy turned her eyes to the horizon, the lip of darkness beyond sight.

Some questions are better left unasked.

Sketchy steered the minivan with his left hand. His elbow dangled outside the window. In his right hand, he held the shotgun flat against his shoulder. The gun's stock dug into his thigh. The red handkerchief was wrapped around his neck.

Now, Sketchy really did look like a cowboy. Maybe one that rides shotgun on a stagecoach. But if he was a cowboy, he'd lost his hat and his hair was mussed and there was a look in his eye that shone like madness.

He slapped the knob to turn on the minivan's radio and flipped to the hard rock station—it came in full of static, but Sketchy wanted some furious bar chords to pound his ears. He could hear that, so it was all good. He smashed his lips together and tasted dust. An unquenchable, ravenous thirst for beer came over him and he groaned.

The Harley's taillight faded from view, but Sketchy kept his eyes along the eastern horizon. He knew the hippie stayed somewhere along that stretch of The Mesa—hell, everybody knew it. But he didn't know where to turn, what dirt road he should take to the hippie's camp. He waited for the quick flash of a head-light, the red cigarette burn of a taillight in the distance.

Anything to give him direction.

Should have fired earlier, might have got him right there in the road. But Sketchy also knew it'd be safer to shoot a man on a back trail somewhere. All he had to do was fire, watch the hippie bleed into the dirt. Then he could turn around and head home. Simple—the mangy coyotes would do the rest. Gypsy, though, she'd taken Sketchy by surprise tonight. He skids to a stop and there she is, riding on the hippie's back like he's some kind of teenage god or something. That fucker has some balls. Sketchy had to give him that…Things had gotten out of hand between Sketchy and Gypsy. They were together for seven years—a good stretch, or so Sketchy thought. But one day she just up and leaves? How the hell does that work? Then he was alone out there in the desert. Only one to keep him company was that sorry-sack school teacher.

And now, he runs into Gypsy on the back of the hippie's bike.

The same fucker who burned down his bar. The whole scene was downright evil. No other way to de-scribe it. Sketchy scanned the horizon again. He'd removed his dark sunglasses but he still couldn't see much. The beer thirst rose in his throat again. He checked his eyes in the rearview mirror—wild and yellow—and smiled at the madness he saw in his reflection. Beer comes later. Now, you need some revenge. Sketchy flipped his gaze back to the horizon and there it was, a soft white glint in the distance, a lone headlight bouncing along a far ridge. It bobbed like a firefly above black water.

Sketchy grinned. One mile ahead was an unmarked dirt road.

He knew just where to turn.

Back at camp, Packard threw a beige cover over the Harley. He scoured the dirt with a flashlight beam and, satisfied they were alone, gave Gypsy the grand tour. He pointed at each section of the camp. "Tent. Fire. Stove. And over there, down that trail, you can pee." He switched off the flashlight and they stood in darkness. A few ghostly howls bounced through the canyon— coyotes on the prowl.

"Nice place you got here." A little sarcasm seasoned her words.

"It's peaceful. That's pretty much all that matters."

"I can see that," she said. "My place has a pool though."

"And you said Mr. Shotgun knows where you stay."

"Yes. Sketchy knows where to find me."

"So, here we are." Packard walked to his Harley and lifted the beige cover, pulled the bottle of bourbon from a saddlebag.

They sat near the fire ring and passed the bottle back and forth.

Gypsy drank more than Packard—he wasn't surprised.

"You're the one who burned down the bar," she said.

Packard didn't answer. He swigged from the bottle and squinted at the night. He swore to himself he'd seen a pair of headlights bouncing out there in the desert.

No, couldn't be...That's your brain giving you an illusion.

More to drink. Less to think. He turned his eyes to Gypsy.

She said, "You burned it to the ground, but why?"

"I didn't like something I heard him say."

"That's all it takes for you? An insult?"

"So much more than that. They tell you who they are by what they say. That's how you know the truth—you listen."

The bottle moved between them.

Gypsy crossed and uncrossed her legs. She huddled in the chair. Packard brought a wool blanket from the tent and she wrapped herself in it. "How long have you been here?"

More bourbon for him. Hot liquid in the throat. Fire in the stomach. "I come now and then. I bounce from here to there, there to here." He didn't expect her to understand.

"I understand," she said.

He looked at her once more. Brown curls fell down her pale neck. Red colored her cheeks. She scratched an eyebrow. Packard's eyes followed the delicate ridge of her nose, trailed to her mouth. *Will she be a wall of wind behind which is emptiness? You fool. You aimless fool.* "He didn't have very good aim," Packard said.

They laughed together.

"I think he fired way too late."

"Times like that, I'm happy to have a little luck." Packard swept his eyes across the desert again. Was that a light? Maybe. No. Back to Gypsy. Back to brown curls and soft skin and eyes that pooled against the night. Memories surfaced in Packard. He heard a voice—sing-songy and velvet—speak his name. Packard. Hey, honey. Glad you're home early. He saw a flash of cream-white skin, sensed the delicate touch of finger-nails and tasted mint. He felt the firm press of a soft wet mouth on his chin—the woman…She was gone now. And how he thought of her that way—the woman— made him feel alone, lost, evil. People die. We're organ-isms and that's all. Packard swallowed more bourbon.

"Where are you?"

Packard looked at Gypsy. He had no answers to these questions. There were only the obvious facts. "I'm here, right here with you." And he added: "I'm drunk a little bit."

Gypsy's teeth flashed. She pushed the blanket away and stood. "Good. So am I." She moved toward him and her body dropped against his, crumbled into him. Her skin was smooth fabric and static crackling. Her lips soft and wet. Packard couldn't escape his own thoughts, but he pressed his palms against the firm surface of Gypsy's back and pulled.

Sketchy parked the minivan where the road dead-ended and the single-track trail slanted toward the canyon. He studied the tire marks that ran both directions—into and out of the high rock walls. He dragged his index finger through the tracks and, with rickety letters in the sand, he wrote: "fuck u." *The hippie camps here, and I'm going to kill him.* Sketchy sensed Gypsy's presence also. He always knew when she was near him. Some kind of extra sense he had, a thing that put him on edge around town. Imagine, walk into a store and know, right away, that your ex-wife was about to turn the corner. Good riddance. Her too. Get rid of them. He rested the shotgun on his shoulder and started down the trail. A small part of him felt nostalgic for the Winchester and wished he could shoot it. Not worth taking the chance. The shotgun barely needed aiming. Hell, point it in the general direction and you'd hit your target. Sketchy needed a sure thing. After a hundred yards, he stopped and listened. Regular desert noise; a soft buzz from insects, wispy plants brushing against each other. Inside him, a small seed of doubt sprouted, broke free, grew into his throat. He wondered if he'd squeeze the trigger. He wondered if he'd freeze, if he'd feel himself seize like an engine run dry. Sketchy lowered the shotgun and looked at it. It was heavy and oily and black. In his mind, Sketchy saw the shiny green watermelon exploding. All the blood-pink pulp and green shell pieces fell around him, a juicy mess in the dirt. It's like that. Like shooting a watermelon. Sketchy rested the shotgun on his shoulder, squinted into the darkness and started down the trail.

Tell yourself the truth.

You live here, in this camp, because you have no more courage, no more life in you to face the world. You've given everything to the road. The only place that forgives is this desert, and it expects nothing from you. That is the gift. The gift of expecting nothing. The gift draws you to this place. Oh, the sand and the rocks and the jagged mountains standing guard—they stand between you and...it. These mountains are your sentries to the world. Tell yourself the truth about your life. The truth about how every moment was once golden, pure white, and filled with joy. Tell about how everything went as planned, until it didn't.

Tell yourself about the woman you loved. She died, you say. She died.

Tell yourself the truth.

Packard saw himself rising in the early morning. He saw himself walking through a city, wading against a sea of people in dark suits and knee-length dresses. He saw himself standing in front of young people, speaking to them. Names burst from his lips in passionate whispers, whispers resounding like gunshots. Then he saw himself in the white, glaring haze of a hospital. He heard voices and beeps and the constant ticking of mysterious machines.

This dream, the dream that never died, came to him night after night.

Packard's eyes opened. His smoky blue irises scanned for shadows through the tent wall. A car door slammed. Far off, footsteps and labored breathing floated across the still air. Packard's hand snaked to Gypsy's warm, bare skin. She woke and her eyes grew wild and frantic when he placed a hand over her mouth.

He whispered, "Somebody's here. Be quiet." Packard took his hand away and felt for the Colt .45 shoved into his boot among the coiled necks of his dirty socks. He curled his fingers around the gun and brought it out, pointed the barrel straight at the tent's low-hanging ceiling.

You know it's Mr. Shotgun. There's nobody else. You know.

Packard wiggled out from beneath the sleeping bag and pulled on his black leather vest. He set the gun down and shoved his legs into his Levis. Gypsy lifted the gun and stared at it. Packard buckled his Levis and took the gun from her. Again, he whispered, "I'm going out there—stay here." He unzipped the tent and crawled into the dark.

The light scrape of footsteps floated down the trail. Mr. Shotgun made no effort to be silent. Packard's eyes adjusted to the darkness. The moon was obscured by cloud cover, but the desert glowed as if beneath diffused candle light. The voice came to him as he was about to stand.

"Leave that pistol in the dirt. And get your ass up."

Packard stopped. He was halfway outside the tent, crawling on all fours. "She's inside," he said. "Don't shoot me here."

"Get up." Sketchy's thin figure appeared from the darkness.

From inside, Gypsy said, "Don't shoot me, I have to work tomorrow."

"You get out of there." Sketchy jabbed the shotgun at Packard. "Stand up and move back."

Packard stood, took a few backward steps. He left the .45 in the dirt. He ran his eyes over the pistol, but knew it would stay there until all this was done. *Should have kept watch. You let the booze and the girl get you good.*

Gypsy crawled out behind him on all fours. She stood and smirked at Sketchy. Her black polo shirt was untucked and her feet were bare below her Levis. "You gonna pull some stupid stunt?" She pulled strands of brown hair from her face.

Sketchy swept his eyes over the camp. "This is some classy shit."

Gypsy shrugged. "It's the company you keep."

Sketchy swung the shotgun toward Packard and started, at the same time, walking toward the man. Packard moved backwards at the same pace as Sketchy.

"Stop fucking moving." Sketchy's hands trembled and the shotgun shook. "Just stay where you are." He stomped past the tent and Gypsy—her sweet juniper scent taunted him—and moved toward Packard. "Stay right there, hippie. Don't move or I swear to God."

Packard stopped and found himself at the edge of the drop-off, where the camp ended and the land careened down into the narrow canyon.

Sketchy gave a brief tug on the red handkerchief tied around his neck. He gripped the shotgun tighter and let it pivot slowly upward to Packard's head.

Packard's eyes, for just a second, glanced over the side. It seemed higher than he'd thought.

Sketchy edged toward the drop-off. He peered over the side—the shotgun pointed at Packard still—and smiled. "You won't make it," he said. "Not a damn chance."

Packard's face showed nothing. His eyes simply pointed at Sketchy—two long dark barrels aimed at the man. In his head, Packard heard Sketchy's voice: *His kind ain't allowed in here.*

Sketchy shook the shotgun. "I want to know why

you burned my place down. Tell me."

Packard said, "A thing worth hating is a thing worth burning."

"What's that from?"

"It's not from anything."

"That bar was all I had," Sketchy said.

"And it wasn't worth a damn thing."

"What the hell do you know?"

"I know what I see," Packard said.

"Damn you. You'll see the other side and—"

Gypsy slammed into him as he said it. Sketchy went over the side. He tossed the shotgun and tried to catch air, but there was nothing to hold and he plummeted to the bottom. The hard granite stopped his fall. The shotgun's clatter across the rocks made more noise than Sketchy's body. Gypsy stood above him. Her toes hung over the edge and her chest rose and fell, rose and fell. One of her hands curled into a tiny fist at her side. In the other hand, she held the Colt .45.

Packard didn't look down at the dead man. He stared at the woman on the edge of the drop-off. Brown curls fell down her pale neck. Red bursts colored her cheeks. Packard's eyes drifted from the delicate ridge of her nose to her mouth.

Will she be a wall of wind behind which is emptiness? You fool. You aimless lucky fool. He took two steps toward her, but then he stopped.

Gypsy slowly lifted the pistol and gripped it with both hands. She centered one eye over the barrel and gazed through the sight. Her chest froze mid-breath and she squeezed the trigger twice. The reports sounded through the canyon, booming claps that rang in Packard's head. Sketchy's body jerked twice and lay still. Gypsy lowered the pistol and stared at the dead man. Again, her chest rose and fell, rose and fell. She said, "He better not get up from that."

Masters hobbled along the highway's shoulder. He wasn't sure how far he'd walked, but it seemed to him that the town kept growing more distant. Starlight illuminated the highway. The solid yellow line at the road's center ran to the horizon and disappeared. Masters put one foot in front of the other. The wet spot near his zipper had dried, but there was still a discoloration showing where urine had run down the inside of his leg. He hitched his pants and tried to walk faster. Masters hobbled down into a dip in the highway, crested a low rise. He stopped. Where Sketchy's bar stood only a few nights before, a bare cement foundation reflected moonlight. Charred wood and ash made a hectic skeleton, a bony graveyard of the bar's former self. Masters stared at the carnage. *Too bad. I could use a beer right now.*

Two gunshots echoed from the desert's far reaches. Masters craned his neck to listen, but the echoes died. There were no more shots.

He shoved his hands into the pockets of his khakis and hobbled toward town.

"There she is, right there."

"Yep, and the drifter dropping her off at work. You got to be kidding."

"How else is she supposed to get to town? She can't walk from up that way."

"Both of them being seen together. Don't that make it obvious, who did it?"

"We all know who did it."

"They'll find Sketchy one of these days. Somebody will. I know it."

"Maybe. Maybe not. Hell, it's not like we lost much."

"A shitty bar without a pool table. We lost that."

"Like I said."

"We lost Sketchy. I guess we lost that too."

"Like I said. We didn't lose much. Hell, if you look at it like that, we didn't lose a damn thing. Shit, is that the old Winchester in his bag, the one I sold the other day?"

"Might be."

"I bet he's gonna sell it back to me…"

ACKNOWLEDGMENTS

I want to thank Lesley, my wife, for supporting me in my passions and, most of all, for bringing our little Charlie into the world! I love you both so much! Thanks to the writers and teachers at The University of Texas-El Paso, Antioch University-Los Angeles, and North Carolina Central University. I want to thank Severest Inks for publishing an early version of "Mesa Boys." I have to thank the editors at All Due Respect for working hard to put out amazing books of crime fiction and noir. You all are doing such great work. And, like last time, I have to say thanks to all the crime writers out there who are banging away at story after story…

Matt Phillips lives in San Diego. His books include *Accidental Outlaws*, *Three Kinds of Fool*, *Redbone*, and *Bad Luck City*. He has published crime stories across the web at *Shotgun Honey*, *Near to the Knuckle*, Out of the Gutter's *Flash Fiction Offensive*, *Pulp Metal Magazine*, *Fried Chicken and Coffee*, *Manslaughter Review*, and elsewhere.

MattPhillipsWriter.com

OTHER TITLES FROM ALL DUE RESPECT

See AllDueRespectBooks.com for complete list

By Greg Barth
Selena: Book One
Diesel Therapy: Book Two
Suicide Lounge: Book Three
Road Carnage: Book Four
Everglade: Book Five

By Eric Beetner
Nine Toes in the Grave

By Phil Beloin Jr.
Revenge is a Redhead

By Math Bird
Histories of the
Dead and Other Stories

By Paul D Brazill
The Last Laugh: Crime Stories

By Sarah M. Chen
Cleaning Up Finn

By Alec Cizak
Crooked Roads: Crime Stories
Manifesto Destination

By Pablo D'Stair
and Chris Rhatigan
You Don't Exist

By C.S. DeWildt
Kill 'Em with Kindness
Love You to a Pulp

By Paul Heatley
FatBoy

By Jake Hinkson
The Deepening Shade

By Preston Lang
The Sin Tax

By Marietta Miles
Route 12

OTHER TITLES FROM ALL DUE RESPECT

See AllDueRespectBooks.com for complete list

By Mike Miner
Prodigal Sons

By Mike Monson
A Killer's Love
Criminal Love and Other Stories
Tussinland
What Happens in Reno

By Matt Phillips
Three Kinds of Fool
Accidental Outlaws

By Rob Pierce
The Things I Love
Will Kill Me Yet: Stories
Uncle Dust
Vern in the Heat
With the Right Enemies

By Michael Pool
Debt Crusher

By Chris Rhatigan
Race to the Bottom
Squeeze
The Kind of Friends Who
Murder Each Other

By Ryan Sayles
I'm Not Happy 'til You're
Not Happy: Crime Stories

By Ryan Sayles
and Chris Rhatigan
Two Bullets Solve Everything

By Daniel Vlasaty
A New and
Different Kind of Pain
Only Bones

By William E. Wallace
Dead Heat with the Reaper
Hangman's Dozen

Made in the USA
Columbia, SC
03 August 2021

42875908R00121